"Wherever she goes she spells trouble."

Mary's pronouncement was emphatic. "I don't know Lorraine Jorgens much better than you do," she added, "but I do know she's man mad. Age wouldn't worry her if she thought she'd found the right man, and I've an idea she's got her sights set on Richard."

Patricia gasped. "Richard Horton?" she breathed. "*Our* Richard?"

"Our Richard. What's more, she's jealous of you, my dear."

"But—but that's ridiculous!" Patricia stammered. "I mean—Richard's nice to me, but he sees me as a child. Still, I'd rather he fell for anyone other than Lorraine Jorgens. She'd never make him happy."

"She'd never make any man happy," said Mary. "All I can say is, she's going to set the place by the ears if she stays very long!"

The Quiet Veld

by

JEAN DUNBAR

Harlequin Books

TORONTO • LONDON • LOS ANGELES • AMSTERDAM
SYDNEY • HAMBURG • PARIS • STOCKHOLM • ATHENS • TOKYO

Original hardcover edition published in 1971
by Mills & Boon Limited

ISBN 0-373-01606-9

Harlequin edition published July 1972

Second printing August 1973
Third printing February 1977
Fourth printing September 1977
Fifth printing April 1978
Sixth printing March 1980

For
Flo Booyssen, East London Cape,
who was in on it from
the beginning

Printed in Canada

CHAPTER I

Richard Horton stood at the door of the lounge, looking sourly at the noisy groups inside. This was not, he thought, his kind of hotel. Although he was a wealthy man, he did not necessarily prefer the larger, more opulent hotels when he was away from home. He liked the simple little country hotels where the rooms were plain but comfortable, the food was plain but well cooked, and the company was good. This place, he thought, was pure bogus as far as he could see. The lounge was decorated with would-be finery, but it was tawdry and shoddy. The lighting was so bad that unless you were sitting right under one of the lights, it would be impossible to read; not that it appeared that anyone used this lounge for reading.

The gayest, noisiest group of people had coalesced under one of the lights, having annexed all the free chairs. Even so, there were not enough chairs for all of them. He caught sight of his stepbrother, Simon Verity, perched on the arm of a chair in which a very pretty girl was sitting. She had unusual coloured hair, neither red, gold nor brown, but with a hint of all three, cut short and curving in just above her ear-lobes, parted in the middle and waving gently from a white, very smooth forehead. She had what all South Africans consider to be an exclusively English complexion, pink and white and clear. Her eyebrows and lashes were much darker than her hair, and when she glanced idly towards the door, he saw that her eyes were large and of an indeterminate opalescent shade, somewhere between blue and green. Tonight, in the frock that she was wearing, they looked sea-green.

She did not, thought Richard, look Simon's usual

type, and yet there were rumours that he was unofficially engaged. Richard did not believe it. Simon was after a job that stipulated that the holder must have a wife for entertaining. He was quite capable of producing a girl as a fiancée, and then, the job in his pocket, announce that the engagement was broken off. A bit hard on the girl, thought Richard, unless of course he had managed to persuade a girl to play the part for the time being. He turned on his heel and went to the reception desk.

'Did you see that young lady?' he asked the girl on late duty. 'The one in green, sitting with that crowd in the lounge, I mean. I suppose you couldn't tell me who she is, could you?'

It was something of a forlorn hope, he thought. So many people must come in here for drinks in the evening. It was a convenient rendezvous, having a good car park and being right on the Main Road.

'Yes, sir,' said the girl. 'You mean the one with the reddish hair? That's Miss Patricia Langdale. She's staying here. She's usually with that young gentleman and a party in the lounge at this time of the evening.'

Richard went back to the door of the lounge. He was teased by something familiar in the girl's face and name. Where had he seen her? Was it in the papers? And he was sure that the name was not Langdale, although it was something like it. What was it? Dale? No, Lang, that was it. He remembered now. She was the stepdaughter of one of the distant Verity connections, who, with his wife, had plunged down the cliff near Whitesand Bay in their car, about six months back. If they had not both been killed outright, the husband, Garth Verity, would have been had up for swindling. There had been several dirty deals put through, and shareholders had lost money. It had cost the firm of Horton and Verity a good deal of money to repay the debts, and it had cost them a great deal of goodwill.

8

Only now were they beginning to get back to something like their old prestige, and that was because of the old reputation of the firm.

There had been one or two photographs of this girl in the papers, but very few. She had not been one of the major protagonists in the affair. Her mother had been an Englishwoman who had married Garth as her second husband. The daughter had been educated in England and had been flown out for the school holidays. Why, Richard asked himself, had Cousin Garth had to do those stupid swindles? Surely there was enough money for him without that?

And what, he asked himself, looking at the girl, was she doing now? Had she no relatives in England that she could go to? Possibly she had been left practically penniless, but surely her mother had had someone who could have sent out the fare? She didn't look the type to fall in with Simon's wildcat schemes, but one never knew. And from her clothes, she hardly looked penniless. Her neatly tailored trouser-suit was ice-blue lurex, more green than blue. Clipped into her ears were heavy, barbaric gilt earrings, and her shoes were gilt sandals with the fashionable heavy heel.

Suddenly she looked round and saw him standing in the doorway staring at her. She said something to Simon who was sitting on the arm of her chair, and he looked up.

'Well, look who's here!' he said. 'Old Sober Dick himself. Come and join us, old horse!'

Richard came into the lounge.

'Meet Pat Langdale, my unofficial fiancée,' said Simon gaily, but with an underlying strain. Where Richard was, there was trouble, at least in his experience.

'I won't join you, thanks,' said Richard quietly. 'I'd like a word with you, though, Simon. In private. It won't take long.'

9

Simon grimaced, but stood up. Sooner or later, one usually did what Dick said. Might as well make it sooner and save trouble.

'Excuse us, Pat, won't you, love?' he said lightly. 'We shan't be long—I hope!'

The girl smiled up at him. 'Of course. I'll be all right.' Her voice, noted Richard, was very English—well-educated English.

'Where can we talk in private?' he asked his step-brother.

'Here, I should think,' said Simon, leading the way beneath an illuminated sign that said 'Verandah Lounge,' to a long, wide, glassed-in verandah, dimly lit and strewn with small tables and chairs. 'It's usually pretty quiet here except on a Saturday night.'

There was not much of a view from the wide windows, especially at this time of the night. The car park lay between them and Main Road, and between them and the sea was a row of flats, houses, shops and hotels that were intersected by little narrow streets.

'Well,' said Simon, dropping down into a chair by one of the tables, 'what did you want to say to me, old chap?' He half rose. 'By the way, what d'you want to drink?'

'Nothing at the moment, thanks.'

'Well, I do.' He went and rang the nearest bell before rejoining his stepbrother. 'Now, what's it all about?'

'What,' asked Richard without further preamble, 'is Miss Patricia Lang doing masquerading as your " un-official " fiancée?'

'Langdale,' corrected Simon, 'and why should you think it's a masquerade?'

'Oh, for heaven's sake!' exclaimed Richard wearily, 'do you think I'm a fool? I recognised the girl from her pictures in the papers. After all, I took a good deal of interest in the case. It was pretty close to me, if you remember. It was connected with the firm. And I shouldn't think you'd get yourself seriously engaged to Miss Lang. She can't be very well off, can she?'

They were interrupted by a waiter coming to take their order.

'Scotch, please, and water and ice. Oh, make it a double, will you? Sure you won't join me, Dick?'

'Quite sure, thank you.' Richard waited until the waiter was out of earshot and then: 'Well?' he went on. 'I'm waiting to hear what role Miss Lang's playing in your affairs.'

'Well, you know I'm after that job of P.R.O. in Capetown,' said Simon. 'The old firm's not too keen on employing another Verity. Can't say I blame them, but they ought to be glad that I'm wanting to settle down to a serious job of work.'

The Capetown offices of Horton and Verity (Pty) Ltd., Manufacturers and Importers of Farm Implements, the headquarters of the firm, was here in Capetown. Richard was in charge of the Eastern Cape branches, but did a good deal of liaison work between the branches. It had been the rumour, brought to Southcliff, on the Eastern Cape Coast, of his stepbrother's engagement that had brought him to headquarters, together with the news, in a letter from his uncle, the Chairman, that Simon was after the job of Public Relations Officer.

'Well,' went on Simon, 'Uncle Chris insisted that the post ought to go to a married man because of the entertaining that goes with the job. I hinted that I was thinking along those lines myself, so then I just had to get hold of a girl who'd pose as my fiancée for long enough to get the job. Pat was down on her luck, so there you are.'

'What's she been doing since her parents died?' asked Richard. The girl didn't look as if she'd been roughing it for the last six months, he thought, but some people always manage to fall on their feet. Probably there had been another mildly dishonest fiddle of some kind to keep her going. Blood will out. Then he remembered that the girl was not Garth Verity's daughter, was no relation at all. It was her stepfather, not her father, who had died before he could face a charge of embezzlement.

'She had a post as companion to an old lady,' said Simon. 'Old Anthony Verity's widow, as a matter of fact. Remember, she married one of the Hugheses of Natal—Evan, I think. Evan died and left the old lady quite well off, and she's been following the sun ever since—summer here in Capetown, winter in Durban.'

'Wasn't she the mother of Tony Verity who got killed in the Congo, leaving a widow and child?' asked Richard. 'If so, I know Mary pretty well, but I didn't know her mother. Mary's married again, too.'

Simon shrugged his shoulders. He wasn't interested. 'I haven't a clue. Anyway, the old dear got in touch with Pat—liked the look of her photograph in the paper, I suppose, and remembered that she was a Verity herself once, or had been married to one.' He broke off to pay the waiter for his drink and went on, 'Pat didn't say so, but maybe she thought that the old girl would leave her something. After all, she was a Verity by marriage before she went and got hitched to old Hughes. No such luck. There was no Verity money there; apparently Garth was never very well lined. And old Mrs Hughes only had the usufruct of the Hughes money. On her death, it all reverted to an old Hughes cousin somewhere near Pietermaritzburg. Poor old Pat was left out on a limb for the second time in one year.'

'So you've taken her in and let her think she's marrying you, have you? What's she going to feel like when she knows you're only using her?' Richard's voice was quiet but scathing.

'What an opinion you have of me, Dick!' Simon was full of injured innocence. 'As if I'd do anything like that! What makes you think I'm not intending to marry Pat? She's a very nice girl; darn pretty, too.'

'I know you, Simon,' said his stepbrother. 'You'll never let yourself get tied up to a girl without money. And why the false name?'

Simon, as usual, gave in. Richard, he thought, could make rings round him any time.

'Pat's in it for a bit of money while she looks round,' he said. 'She knows quite well that there's no question of marriage. The unofficial engagement lasts until I'm well and truly settled in the job, and then, instead of being made official, it's broken off by mutual consent. And as for now, I'm paying Pat enough for the deception, to pay for a room here, and leave enough over for pocket money. She doesn't need clothes; she's got enough to last her for years. Don't forget, her old man was wealthy until he took to crime and got caught out.'

'Of course,' said Richard, 'there won't be any question of your getting the P.R.O. job after what you've told me tonight.'

Simon shrugged. 'I might have known you'd take it this way. What brings you to Capetown anyway? You ought to be sitting in Southcliff or Port Elizabeth like a spider in its web!'

'I came because one of the travellers had heard a rumour that you were engaged or about to become engaged, and at the same time, I had a letter from Uncle Chris saying that you'd applied for the P.R.O. job, and did I think it would be wise to employ you? It was, he told me, a job intended for a married man, but you'd hinted that you had leanings towards matrimony. He was a bit dubious about taking another Verity into the firm; the Verity men haven't shown themselves very stable over the years. He said he'd defer to my judge-

13

ment.'

Simon sneered, ' And what did the little paragon say?'

' I wrote and said that I thought he was right to feel doubtful, and that if he could hold on, I'd come to Capetown and see for myself what was going on.'

' It's all wrong!' Simon burst out. ' It's damned unfair. It's a family firm, isn't it? Horton and *Verity*? There've been Veritys in the firm ever since it was founded eighty years ago. A Verity shouldn't have to be vetted to see if he's suitable; he ought to be *in* the firm. In it by right.'

' He *ought* to,' said Richard dryly. ' Unfortunately, so many of the Verity men seem to be unreliable that we have to vet them before we let them in. Look at Garth. And old Anthony never did much—he could never keep money. He married that half-French wife and gambled everything away. His son Tony was a bit of a rolling stone—travelling for the firm for a year or two, then got fed up and got taken on on a tramp steamer, came back and travelled for half a dozen other firms and wasn't satisfactory with any of them, then went up to the Congo as a mercenary and got killed, leaving a wife and teenage daughter. Mary was a nursing Sister, and worked to keep Toinette, the daughter, and old Mrs Verity looked after the child and kept house for them, until she married Evan Hughes and went off to live in Durban. Then Mary took up private nursing so that she could be at home during the child's school holidays. That was how she met her second husband, Charles Milstead.'

' I seem to know that name,' said Simon.

' You ought to. He's the son of the late G.O.C. Milstead, the naturalist, who wrote a good many standard textbooks in between expeditions. Charles used to go with him as illustrator. He's no mean artist. Then Charles got severely injured and they had to give up.

Since then, Charles has been producing charmingly illus-trated books—one can hardly call them textbooks, they're too entertaining—on South African birds, illus-trated with his own watercolours. Done very well out of them. Mary nursed him while he was getting over his injury.

'Now they live in their old family house in Blouvlei. Martha's kids are with them at the moment. Trouble is, I can't leave them there indefinitely; it's not fair to Mary. What with Charles, who's still not too robust, and her daughter by Tony Verity, and a six-months-old baby of Charles's, she has her hands full without three of someone else's kids.'

Martha was Richard's sister. She had married a scientist who had been killed in the Antarctic. Taking the car out one evening, she had skidded on a patch of gravel on an untarred stretch of road just outside the little village of Blouvlei, turned the car over, and been killed instantly. There had, at the time, been some doubt as to whether to call the tragedy accidental death or suspected suicide, since it had occurred shortly after she had received the news of her husband's death, but no one who knew the cheerful and courageous Martha Horton had entertained the idea of suicide for a second.

'Hmm! Our family does seem to have had its share of mishaps and tragedies lately, hasn't it?' mused Simon. 'What are you going to do about the kids?'

'I haven't an idea—at least I have, but don't know how to implement it. You know Number Five, Green Street—the one next door to the Milsteads'—is Horton property. A great-uncle of mine lived there for years. Since he died, it's been let to a series of tenants. At the moment it's been empty for about two months, but the agents say it's in good enough repair. If I could put the kids there, with someone reliable to look after them, Mary and Charles would be next door to keep an eye on them, but they'd be out of Mary's hair. Not that she ever grumbles, but it can't be much fun to have three of someone else's children when you've enough to cope with in your own family.'

'I know.' Simon spoke as one coming up with a brilliant idea. 'Pat'll be out of a job now that you've rumbled our little deception. How about giving her the job?'

Richard stared at him. 'You've got to be joking! I said someone *reliable*. Besides, why isn't she in a decent job herself by now? She's spent six months trailing round after an old lady and now she's being paid to help you to deceive the firm into giving you a job. She's had six months to find something. What's wrong with her? Or does she take after her stepfather—caught his little tricks?'

'No-o.' Simon spoke thoughtfully. 'I don't think she's much like old Garth somehow. But look at it this way, Dick. The kid was always brought up to think she was going to be a poor little rich girl. She wasn't trained for a job. She was sent over to an expensive boarding school in England, stayed with her grandmother—a very old-fashioned old lady, from what Pat says—at weekends and at Easter, when the holiday wasn't long enough for her to fly out, and when she didn't get her Matric. or whatever it is that they pass in the U.K. when they leave school, Mummy said it didn't matter after all, as she'd never have to earn her own living. She's no fool, but she hasn't an idea how to keep herself. Doesn't know enough to come in out of the rain.'

Richard smiled a little grimly. 'So it seems, since she was silly enough to take up with you, and come into one of your mad schemes. I think I'd better have a talk with the young lady.'

'Don't take it out on her too much, Dick. I talked her into it. She'd never have agreed if she hadn't been pretty desperate.'

Richard raised his eyebrows. It almost sounded as if Simon was a bit taken with the girl. Still, she'd looked attractive enough, the little that he had glimpsed of her, sitting there in the lounge.

'I'll treat her like a crate of eggs,' he promised, sarcastically. 'Go and fetch her here, Simon.'

Patricia was laughing at something that one of the others had said when Simon went into the lounge to call her, but there was a brittleness, an underlying strain in her manner. Simon had mentioned his stepbrother Richard to her, and had said that he was simply not with it. He had also said that it was very hard to put anything across Richard. She felt cold. By now, she thought, Richard would know all about the deception against which she had fought at first, but had finally agreed to because she was desperate, and needed the money. She looked round when she heard Simon's whistle from the door.

'Oy!' he called. 'Here a sec, Pat.'

She got up and went over to him, her drink in one hand, a cigarette in a long amber holder in the other. She looked the picture of sophistication instead of the unhappy, worried, bewildered girl that she really was.

'What is it, Simon?' she asked. 'What did he want?'

'He's seen through our little deception, sweetie. He saw at once that there was something phoney about it. One of the travellers talked—asked him if he'd heard I was getting engaged. Damned travellers! I might have known one of them would gossip. At the same time, Uncle Chris wrote and told him I was applying for the P.R.O. job. Wanted to know if Dick thought I was the right person for the job or something.'

'What did you tell him? Richard, I mean?'

'I tried to stall him off, but you don't know our Dick. Now he wants a word with you, my sweet.'

'With—with me? What does he want with me? What'll he say to me?'

Simon laughed. 'Don't worry, sweetie, he can't eat you. He'll probably read you a lecture on the error of your ways and he might even find out how you're placed. I just hinted that his stopping our scheme would put you in a very awkward position financially.'

'Oh, Simon, how could you? Now he'll think that because my stepfather was a Verity, I want to sponge on the firm—think it owes me something.'

'Don't be daft.' Simon took her elbow. 'Come on, he's waiting. And remember, although he's a bit of an old stick-in-the-mud, he's a decent enough old horse at heart.'

As Simon propelled her into the chilly, dimly-lit verandah lounge, Patricia did not feel particularly reassured.

Richard rose at their approach. Patricia could not see him clearly, but she had the impression of a hawk-like profile, smooth dark hair and a firm jaw. She wondered what colour his eyes were; you couldn't see in this light, but they seemed to be rather light and very bright. As they came up to him, he smiled a little, showing very white teeth.

'Good evening, Miss Lang. I'm Simon's stepbrother, Richard Horton. Yes, I'm afraid he's told me all about your—shall we say your association? Don't blame him too much, though. I practically forced it out of him. I'd like a talk with you, if you don't mind. Alone.' He shot a glance at Simon, who began to vanish in the direction of the door.

Patricia felt hollow, and then suddenly remembered that the hollowness could be from hunger as well as from apprehension.

'Do you mind if I go back to the lounge and eat first?'

she asked. 'One of the others went out for sausage rolls and chips before the shops shut. I promise I won't run away.' Somehow, she summoned a smile as she looked up at him.

'Haven't you eaten?' Richard looked at his watch. 'But it's nearly half past nine!'

'I—I suppose we forgot the time.'

'But you're staying here. Why don't you eat in the dining-room?'

'None of the others is staying here, and the dining-room's pretty grim if one's on one's own. It's far more cosy to eat meat pies and chips in the lounge with a crowd.'

Richard glanced at the glass in her hand. 'Not very wise to eat so late when you spend the evening drinking, is it?'

Patricia laughed, a rather wry little laugh. It had a brittle sound.

'Oh, I can make one John Collins last the whole evening,' she said, showing him her quarter-full glass. 'It's a trick I learned when I wasn't able to pay my way at a party.'

'Hmm! I apologise. You show some sense. It seems that you've been through a very thin time, and that you were singularly ill-equipped to cope with it. It's no wonder, really, that you got caught up in Simon's mad schemes. Well, I'd better take you out somewhere to get a bite. Go and get a coat or something.'

In a very short time she reappeared, a chinchilla cape over her shoulders. It was already spring, but the October evening had turned chilly. Richard looked down at her ironically.

'I'm surprised you're not wearing mink,' he said.

Patricia appeared not to notice the sarcasm.

'I did have a mink cape,' she said, 'but I sold it when the crash came. I suppose I ought to have sold this too, but it seemed too hard to let *everything* go all at once.'

It was so evident that she was being truthful and neither sarcastic in her turn nor bitter that Richard said nothing, but propelled her through the glass front door to the car park, and to a staid-looking Wolseley, which he unlocked and helped her in.

Surprised that he was not driving a Volvo or something high-powered like an E-type Jaguar, at first, Patricia did not notice where they were going. She had always thought of a Wolseley as a family car— not for a poor family, but not the type of car that she would have thought Simon's stepbrother would drive. He was the big boss of the whole Eastern Cape complex of Horton and Verity. She would have thought that his car would be more of a status symbol.

She became aware that they were driving towards Capetown, away from Sea Point, and that they were passing Green Point Common. As she was wondering where they were going, Richard swung the car down to the right, towards the sea. Now she knew. This winding road led to the Doll House, a drive-in café which was open late, and which served delicious coffee and sandwiches.

'If there'd been a fog,' said Richard, pulling up in the car-park outside the brightly-lit little building, 'I'd have had to think of somewhere else. Mouille Point foghorn's a bit of a deterrent to serious conversation.'

As he spoke, the car was flooded with light from the beam of the gay red and white lighthouse just across the road from where they were. Before it moved on, she caught a half-smile on his face, a glimpse of humour. If Simon hadn't so often complained that his stepbrother had no sense of humour, she would not have been surprised.

'I thought this was a sound idea,' he said. 'It's a

bit late to get dinner anywhere, and one can get reasonable privacy in a car, which one can't at some of those restaurants that stay open all night.' He flashed his headlights to attract the attention of a waiter, and waited until Patricia had finished eating the very satisfying chicken sandwich that he brought before he started to speak.

' Had enough?'

' Plenty, thanks.'

' Sure? More coffee?'

' We-ell. . . .' In spite of the fur cape, the evening was chilly, a damp wind blowing from the nearby Atlantic.

' Go on,' said Richard. ' I'm going to.'

When they were both sipping the fragrant, steaming coffee from thick cups, he turned to her. Now for it, she thought, her heart sinking.

' Now,' he said, ' tell me why you got yourself into such a ridiculous pickle. Don't you know you could get yourself into serious trouble, going round under an assumed name, pretending to be someone else's fiancée? You knew, I suppose, that it was only a temporary arrangement?'

' Yes, I knew.' Her voice was dreary.

' You're not in love with Simon?' Richard's voice was full of concern. ' I mean, you didn't have any hopes that he might change his mind and marry you after all—make the engagement fact as well as pretence?'

' No,' she said. ' I didn't expect Simon to change his mind. I'm not naïve enough for that. I'm not in love with him or anything.'

' Then why?'

Patricia put her empty cup carefully down on the tray that was clipped on to the edge of the open car window.

' Mr Horton,' she said, ' I don't expect you to understand this, but I was desperate. When I met Simon coming out of the attorney's office that morning, I didn't know where to turn.'

'What were you doing at the attorney's?'

'I'd gone to see if there wasn't something—just a few rands, left over from the crash—something to tide me over until I could find another job that a completely unskilled and untrained person could do.'

'And there was nothing?'

'Nothing. Simon was going in, and he recognised me. Wanted to know what I was doing there. I told him, and he said he might have something for me. I must wait. So I waited until he came out; he wasn't long. He took me to tea at the Mount Nelson, and outlined his scheme.

'At first I didn't want anything to do with it; I knew it was dishonest, and I couldn't see how it could work, but Simon talked me into it eventually; I suppose because I *was* so desperate.'

'Yes, I see.' Simon, Richard knew, could be a very persuasive talker when he wished.

'So I just went along with it. After all, it was dishonest, I know, but it wasn't illegal or anything, was it? I mean, we weren't breaking any laws, were we?'

'I'm not so sure about that. I'd have to find out.' Patricia could tell from his voice that he was smiling. Then he became serious. 'But for heaven's sake, why on earth didn't you try to get a proper job? Being a companion to a spoiled old lady—yes, I knew old Mrs Hughes slightly. Her first husband was a Verity—and pretending to be the fiancée of a hare-brained young man so that he can get a job because they think that he'll soon have the wife that's required of him in that job—that's no life for a girl of your age. How old are you, by the way, if it isn't an indiscreet question?'

'Twenty-one. You ask why I didn't go for a decent

job? I'll tell you why.' She turned round in the car to face him, her face, intermittently lit by the beams from the lighthouse, very earnest. 'Have you any idea how difficult it is for someone who hasn't a bean in the world to get a decent job? Everything's skilled nowadays. You can't train for nothing unless you can get bursaries, loans, scholarships. Nearly every good job needs Matric. or Standard Ten. I went to school in England; I've no idea how educated you have to be to have reached your Standard Ten.'

'I didn't even get very good O-levels—they're the ordinary standard that one has to reach in England to get a school-leaving certificate. If you want to go higher, to a university or something, you have to get what they call A-levels.'

Richard nodded. 'Go on.'

'I tried nursing. After all, they pay you while you're training. It sounded just the job. But I found that to train, you've got to have Standard Ten. They told me that there's a two-year training for auxiliaries or something, but even for that, you need Standard Seven. It's hopeless; I don't even know if I'm up to that standard or not. And besides, I was educated in England, like I said, and I can't speak Afrikaans. Everyone wants you to be bilingual, and I never even heard it at home, not even after Mummy married Uncle Garth. She never learned the language, and he spoke English at home, and never worried that I never learned it.

'I tried for a job at the seed factory, but they said I wasn't the type; I'd never stick it. Then, eventually, I *did* nurse. I got a job as a nurse-aide at that nursing home out at Claremont—Hibiscus Lodge. It was there that I met Mrs Hughes. She was recovering from a coronary. She seemed to take a fancy to me, and suggested that I became her companion.

'It was a bit dull, but she was quite sweet, and she

paid well. I know that sounds mercenary, but one tends to panic if one's always had plenty and lands up with nothing, specially if one's got absolutely no qualifications whatsoever. I managed to save a bit, too. I still had plenty of clothes, so that was no expense, and everything was found. But poor Mrs Hughes had another fatal coronary when I'd been with her for six months. I just hadn't saved enough to keep me going until I found another job that was within my capabilities.'

' I suppose you don't know anything about child-care or housekeeping?' was Richard's next surprising question.

' Not much, really. I did a year's domestic science the year I left school, and I often looked after an aunt's young children during the Easter holidays. They were too short for it to be worthwhile flying out to Mummy. That's all.'

' Did you enjoy it? The domestic science and looking after your aunt's children, I mean?'

' Why, yes. Why do you ask?' Surely he wasn't going to offer her a job? But what did he have to do with domestic science and children? Patricia wondered. Simon had always said that his stepbrother was a confirmed bachelor.

' I'm taking you back to the hotel now,' said Richard. ' You're tired. But I'll give you the address of my office, and you must come and see me at eleven o'clock tomorrow morning. I just *might* have something for you. Don't bank on it; it's only a vague possibility, but it's an idea.'

CHAPTER II

The next morning, after a somewhat sleepless night, Patricia was in Capetown far earlier than she need have been. She could not afford a taxi and one never knew how long one would have to wait for a bus. She walked up Adderley Street slowly, to use up the time, and then, as she still had more than half an hour to wait, and the offices of Horton and Verity were only a few minutes' walk away, went into the Koffiehuis in the Grootekerk-gobbou. The coffee room was fairly large, light and airy, but had an intimate air. Over a pot of tea, she mused on what Richard Horton might have to offer her.

Why had he asked if she knew anything about house-keeping and children? Was he really going to offer her a job—she who was completely untrained, and virtually a stranger in the country? She realised now that she had never really settled down as a South African, although, being the daughter and stepdaughter of South African citizens—for her mother had become naturalised when she married Garth Verity, and he had legally adopted his wife's daughter—she knew little of the country beyond her own small circle in Capetown, and little really of that. Until three years ago, when she was eighteen, she had spent all the English school terms in Cheltenham, living with her grandmother and going to the College there as a day-girl. That meant that for the greater part of the year, she was out of the country in which, technically, she was a resident. As she stayed in England for the short Easter holiday, and only flew out to the Cape for the long summer holiday and at Christmas, it meant that she was even longer in England each year.

It was a pity, she thought, that the long English summer holidays coincided with the chill, rainy Cape winter. Once or twice, her stepfather had taken a long holiday in the winter and had flown with his wife and stepdaughter to Amanzimtoti on the Natal South Coast. Here, although it was chilly sometimes, it was nothing like the English winter, and as often as not, the days were far more warm and sunny than those of an English summer.

She had loved the far shorter Christmas holidays, the sunny Cape Christmas, the Coon Carnival on New Year's Day, the squirrels in Government Avenue, so tame that they would take peanuts from your hand, and the cheerful Cape Coloured peanut vendor at the gate.

There had been long days out of doors, too; drives round the glorious Cape Peninsula, out of Baauwberg Bay on the bare Atlantic coast to the north of Capetown where the white sands were buffeted by the great white combers, and across tumbling blue waters Capetown lay, sprawled around the foot of Table Mountain. There were days when they went swimming in the big open-air pool at Sea Point, not far from where she was now staying, drives up the mountain, and out to the wine farms of Groote Constancia and Alphen—show places of an earlier and more gracious age.

She could remember driving out to Hermanus, a fishing village that had become a seaside resort between the mountains and the sea, and had stopped to picnic high above the sea on a mountain pass—what was its name? —Houwhoek, that was it.

She wondered why Richard Horton wanted to see her. There had been no sign of Simon last night when Richard had taken her back to her hotel—not of Simon nor of any of the crowd. She wondered why the party had broken up so early, for it was early for them. She had arrived back at a little after eleven o'clock, and often the crowd kept it up long after the bar had closed.

She glanced at her watch. There were only ten minutes left before she had to be at the Horton and Verity offices in Longmarket Street. She got up, smoothed down her skirt and went to pay her bill.

It was not quite eleven when she came to the tall grey building. Richard had said go straight up to the third floor. She found that the only thing on the ground floor, apart from the foot of the stairs, was the lift, so she pressed the button. The lift seemed nearly as old as the building, rickety and noisy, but it carried her up safely enough.

There was a bare passageway, and a doorless opening a little way down. Painted on the white walls was a pointing hand, with the legend: *To the offices of Horton and Verity, (Pty). Ltd. Manufacturers and Importers of Farming Implements.* She went along, following the pointing painted finger, and found herself in a large room, on one side of a counter behind which there were about a dozen girls at desks, all typing away for dear life.

Patricia did not know whether to speak, and if so, what to say, to knock on the counter, or to cough. She was saved from her dilemma when one of the typists looked up from her desk and saw her, and stopped typing to walk over to the counter.

' Did you want to see someone?'

' Yes—er—Mr Horton. Mr Richard Horton,' said Patricia, a sinking feeling at the pit of her stomach.

' I'm afraid he can't be seen at this time without an appointment,' the girl said, with an air of slight insolence that annoyed Patricia, who not so long ago had been accustomed to very different treatment. She had, in the last six months, almost forgotten what it had been like to be spoiled, cosseted and treated as a privileged person. Now, in the knowledge that she had a right to be where she was, something of her old poise returned. She knew that she was impeccably turned out; her crimplene two-piece was in a soft leaf-green that suited her to perfection. Her tan shoes, gloves and handbag were just the right shade to set it off, and furthermore, they were nearly the same colour as her bright hair. Hardly any of the clothes that she had had in the old life were worn out. She had had little opportunity of wearing them much during the past six months. She felt that she looked just right this morning, neat and smart, but that she had not overdone it.

She did not wear the barbaric, chunky earrings this morning. In her ears were a small pair of topaz and silver studs. All the good jewellery that she had possessed—her Lang grandmother's pearls and the good jewellery that her stepfather had given her for birthdays and Christmas when she was old enough to wear it, and which he had insisted that his adopted daughter ought to wear in public—had been sold off to pay debtors.

Now, drawing herself up, she looked the typist in the eye.

'I have an appointment,' she said, producing the business card that Richard had given her the previous evening. 'My name's Lang; Miss Patricia Lang. Mr Horton asked me to be here at eleven o'clock this morning. Will you find out if he can see me, please.'

The girl muttered an apology, gave Patricia a curious look and went off. Patricia noticed that she was the recipient of interested looks from the other girls, some of whom had stopped typing and had been frankly listening to the conversation. With difficulty, Patricia managed to control her rising colour. Too many of those curious stares had come her way six months ago, but insulated in the self-effacing position of companion to old Mrs Hughes, she had received little curiosity since then.

She found that she disliked it now as little as she had done immediately after the death of her mother and stepfather. She wondered if it was mere inquisitiveness at the appearance of an unexpected and not very businesslike-looking visitor at that hour of the morning, or if any of them had seen her picture in the papers at the time of the crash, remembered it, and recognised her.

Her speculations were cut short by the reappearance of the girl, who said, ' Just go that way, please. Yes, straight through that door,' before sitting down once more behind her desk and going on with her work.

Patricia noticed that there was an open door on the other side of the room, where the girl had indicated. Holding herself proudly upright, she marched over to it, and knocked on the door. A woman's voice said, ' Come in !'

Patricia found herself in yet another outer office, but this time there was only one desk. There was an older woman sitting at it, a well-groomed, attractive woman. She stood up as Patricia came in.

' Miss Lang? If you'll take a seat, I'll see if Mr Richard's ready for you.' She went and knocked at the —this time closed—door on the other side of this room. Patricia sat down on a small armchair with wooden arms beside a small, low round table on which there were what she took to be magazines, but when she picked up one or two, she found that they were mostly reports on the progress of the firm, and that even the one or two colourful ones were catalogues of farming equipment— tractors, disc-ploughs, electric shears, sprinklers. For lack of anything more interesting, she was glancing through one of these when the secretary came back.

' Will you go in now, please, Miss Lang?' She stood at the open door of the office, holding it open for Patricia. Richard's voice came through: ' Come in, Miss Lang. Thank you, Miss van Deventer. I'll ring if there's anything I want.'

Patricia went in, and Richard rose from behind a large desk to greet her.

Patricia's first impression was that he was not as tall as she had thought him last night. Of course, the glimpse that she had had as he had stood at the door of the lounge had been deceptive; she had been sitting down and he had been standing, so that he would have seemed taller than in fact he was. In the dimness of the verandah lounge, he had seemed to loom and tower over her, but the light had been bad, and she had been even more nervous than she was now. Even so, he was no dwarf. If he was not six foot, he must have been about five foot ten or eleven. Patricia was five foot six.

Her second impression was that his eyes, which she had thought lightish the previous evening, were a very bright hazel, and his hair, which she had thought black in the poor lighting, was really dark brown. His face was slightly sunburned as though he spent a good deal of his time in the open air. His hand too, when he came round the desk to shake hers with a firm grip, was brown.

'Good morning, Miss Lang. Sit down.' He indicated a comfortable chair and Patricia sat down, facing him across the desk. She was surprised to realise, now that she had got her breath, that he was treating her courteously, almost as if she might be a client.

'Now, Mis Lang,' he said, crossing his hands on the desk before him and leaning forward over them, 'I don't know how you're going to like my suggestion, and I'm not at all sure that I'm being wise to make it, but I've often found that it pays to play one's hunches. But first, I'd like to ask you a few questions about yourself. Don't think I'm being idly curious; it's merely that when one's about to offer someone a position, it's natural to want to know, as far as possible, if they can fill it.'

'But I told you last night,' said Patricia, 'I'm not

30

equipped to fill any position.'

The little crinkles round his eyes deepened as he smiled —a charming smile, Patricia noticed. She began to wonder if Simon had been strictly accurate when he described his stepbrother as a stuffed shirt.

' Now, tell me,' he said. ' This domestic science that you spoke of last night—what was it, a school course in cookery and needlework?'

' Oh, more than that,' said Patricia. ' I took a course in household management at a College of Domestic Science in Gloucester, not far from Cheltenham, where I stayed with my grandmother while I was at school. Granny insisted on it. She knew that here in South Africa I got no experience in how to do anything in the house at all, and she said that if I ever married an Englishman, I'd be useless, and that she was too old and tired now to teach me.' Her face was saddened for a moment. ' She died soon after I came out here to live. I found her a bit of a strain to live with; she was old-fashioned even for her age, but I was fond of her. She was very good to me.'

Richard interrupted her gently, ' What did this course consist of?'

' Oh, cookery—mostly plain, but we did a bit of high-class cookery at the end of the course. Needlework— plain and fancy, laundry, housewifery, hygiene and a little elementary anatomy and physiology, and the course included the first Red Cross examinations in First Aid and Home Nursing. Oh, and there was a little very elementary book-keeping, and some upholstery. Most of us made humpties, though a few of them brought arm-chairs from home to cover.'

' Humpties?' Richard looked bewildered.

' You know, those little round upholstered stool things. I think some people call them pouffes, though I don't know if that's the correct name for them either.' She smiled at him, beginning to relax. 'And in our last term, we had to spend a fortnight in the little house belonging to the College. Four students and a lecturer lived there—an overflow from the hostel. The first week you did the housework, including waiting at table, and the other girl, who'd already done her stint at the housework, did the cooking, which included all the ordering. Then she went back to ordinary classes and you took over the cooking, and someone else came and did the housework.'

'Hmm! Sounds fairly comprehensive. And you say you helped with your aunt's children. How much time did you spend with them? And what ages were they?'

'Aunt Catherine lived next door to Granny. She had two children by the time I was fifteen, and another born the following year. It was during the Easter holidays, and they came to stay with Granny while Aunt Cath was in the nursing home, and I had to look after them and try to keep them quiet. Robina was ten and Bobby seven. I often used to give a hand with them and the baby at weekends too, when I hadn't got too much homework. Not so comprehensive, I'm afraid, but fun all the same.'

'Yes . . . well.' Richard surveyed her from the other side of the large desk, and Patricia wondered if she passed muster, and what was coming next. 'I don't know if you'll like what I have to offer. You'd be shut away in a little backveld dorp. I don't know how you'd find it after the gay life you've been accustomed to.'

'My life hasn't been exactly gay for the past six months,' said Patricia somewhat dryly. Richard smiled.

'No more it has. Well, to make you understand what I have to offer, I'll have to put you in the picture. I had a sister Martha, a little older than myself. She was married to a geologist, and they had three children. The eldest, Peggy, is now eleven, the second, David's, six, and the baby, Peter, usually known as Podge, for obvious reasons, is eighteen months old.

'Their father, David Selwyn, was a geologist as I've said, and went out last year for what was supposed to be a year in the Antarctic. He fell on a rockface or ice precipice or something, trying to get down to the rock—I've never been able to get at the details. Shortly afterwards their mother, going for a drive one day, skidded her car on a dirt road in bad weather conditions, and was killed outright.'

Patricia gasped. 'How ghastly!' From her own experience, she knew how the relatives of the dead woman must feel.

'Yes, well, of course there was an inquest, and of course suicide was mentioned, but none of us who knew Martha ever entertained the idea for a moment. She was on the road to a farm belonging to friends, and we thought that she must have suddenly decided to visit them. The children were being looked after by the Milsteads, who live next door.' Richard's tone was unemotional. If anything, it became a little drier than before; that was all.

'It was providential,' he went on, 'that I happened to know the people who lived next door. Mary Milstead's first husband was a Verity—Tony Verity, who, by an odd coincidence, was the son of Mrs Hughes, for whom you've just been working. Tony must have been a rather unsatisfactory husband for Mary. He wasn't as unscrupulous as my stepbrother Simon. No, he wasn't a brother; he was a cousin. The main trouble about him was that he was a rolling stone. He took job after job that took him away from home. Eventually he went up to the Congo as a mercenary, leaving Mary with a daughter of about fourteen.

'She married Charles Milstead, and they're very happy. Not only are he and Mary so much in love that one envies them; he's a wonderful stepfather for Mary's daughter Antoinette. He couldn't be fonder of her than if he were her real father.

'My niece and nephews are, at the moment, planted upon the Milsteads. It comes harder on Mary than on Charles, of course. The woman always has to bear the brunt of that kind of thing. She never grumbles, and they're very happy with her, but it's not fair on her. Her husband's never been strong after a severe accident some years ago, and as well as Toinette, who can, of course, look after herself now, Mary's got a baby of about Podge's age. Obviously, I can't leave them there indefinitely, and I've been casting about to find someone to look after them. Now it looks as if I've found her.'

Dumbfounded, Patricia gazed at him across the big desk.

'You—you mean—me?' She was incredulous.

Richard smiled. 'I mean you.'

'But you can't, after I . . .'

'After you tried to pull that silly deception with Simon?' He smiled again. 'I told you I sometimes find it pays to play your hunches. I believed you when you said you only went into it because you were desperate. I think you'll manage all right. I know I'd got someone a little older in mind, but children often get on with someone nearer their own age better than one of these so-called ''motherly'' types who mother them to death. Anyway, you'll have Charles and Mary Milstead next door. They'll help you out in any difficulty. It won't be like having the kids parked on them. And Charles's brother-in-law is one of Blouvlei's two doctors.'

Patricia let out a long breath.

'I simply don't know how to thank you, and after the way I've behaved.'

Richard waved this aside. 'I've told you what I think about that. Now, about salary, and how soon

34

you can start. I'll put a call through to Mary Milstead today and ask her to find a maid to get Number Five cleaned up. It's furnished already.'

In a moment, they were deep in plans.

CHAPTER III

Patricia looked at the countryside whirling past from the upper berth of the second-class compartment as she sipped her coffee. This was no mean feat as the berth was high up, and she had almost to lie flat to see out of the carriage window. They would soon be stopping at Boschfontein, and after that it was only about half an hour's run to Blouvlei. This was a slow train; it had to be or it would not have stopped at a little place like Blouvlei.

She had had to change trains at Cookhouse when it was still dark, but light came early and quickly on late October mornings. Although the shadows were still long in the kloofs that split the mountains, it was already full daylight.

Patricia was glad that it was a warm morning. It had not been worth hiring more bedding at Cookhouse at this late stage of the night, even if it had been possible. She had been shown to the berth of a passenger who had been getting off at Cookhouse.

The train stopped with a series of jerks, and Patricia saw that they were in a small station. Notices, still with the lights burning above them although the sun was already high, said: *Boschfontein*, giving the additional information in small figures underneath that they were three thousand five hundred feet above sea level.

Probably, thought Patricia, they had not got around to changing the feet above sea level to kilometres. She gazed out at the little country station. The buildings were cream-washed, and it all looked very clean. There seemed to be few people about, only a few Africans. There was the sound of clanking milk cans in the not too far distance to remind one that this was dairy farming country. Beyond the station, Patricia could see rolling golden veld, undulating away to distant blue mountains.

She did not know the Eastern Cape well; they had only visited it occasionally when she had been out in South Africa on holiday. She had always thought that she did not like it as much as the Western Cape. The only mountains that came anywhere near the rugged, towering giants of the Western Cape were the mountains round Knysna and George—the Outeniquas—and they were scarcely the Eastern Cape. That part was known as the South Western District.

She had always felt that, compared with the mountains of the Cape, the Groot Drakenstein, the Jonkershoek and Stellenbosch mountains, and the spectacular Hex River Pass, the rolling mountains of the Eastern Cape were dull and insipid; that they lacked interest, being less rugged.

In the same way, she had felt that what she had seen of the Eastern Cape towns was less attractive than Capetown and so very much newer.

From some remote and unknown ancestor, Patricia had inherited a strong feeling for the past. The old buildings in and around Capetown, with their old traditions, and the memories of the first Dutch settlers who had arrived more than three hundred years ago with Jan van Reibeeck, new though they were compared with much that she had seen in England, still breathed of history. Why, much of the Eastern Cape had only been colonised about a hundred and fifty years ago, with the coming of the 1820 settlers. Those who had inhabited the land before that were either tribal Africans, or Trek Boers, nomadic farmers who had built themselves rough homes in the wild and lonely veld.

Patricia remembered visiting Port Elizabeth and East London. Port Elizabeth, a bustling industrial port, had only been a huddle of small houses and a military camp

37

a hundred and fifty years ago when the 1820 settlers had arrived in Algoa Bay, and East London, for all that it was quieter and seemed more settled, was even younger. But Patricia remembered being taken to visit some friends of her stepfather in one of the residential parts of the little city. She had a memory of gracious, low-built, cream-and whitewashed homes, standing in well-tended, flower-bright gardens. There had been about the place an air of continuity, of something going on that had been there for a long time, that was surprising in a place that had barely been in existence a hundred years ago.

Uncle Garth's friend, she remembered, had given her a book to look at—a history in photographs of East London. As short a time ago as 1890, some of the main streets had still looked, in the photographs, as rough and muddy as farm tracks.

Now, she thought that the Eastern Cape might have advantages over the older part of the Republic. Every time she had come back from school during the last few years, she had noticed more and more skyscrapers springing up. The Mother City, which had had such an atmosphere of the past at one time, was becoming engulfed in progress, and except in the suburbs and outskirts, was losing its unique character.

Another thing, she was beginning to be worried by the intermittent, slight, but to her alarming, earth tremors that periodically shook the city since the earthquake that had wrecked so many of the historic old farm homesteads in the Tulbagh district, in the mountains to the north of the city, a year or two back. It would be good to be on stable ground again.

The train started with a jerk, and Patricia resumed her scrutiny of the veld through which they were travelling. The mountains, though for the most part rounded and smooth, had rocky kranzes crowning their summits.

Their flanks were covered with bush, often wild olive, or were gold-green winter grass. Some of them were greener than others, showing that in some places they had already had good spring rains. Lines of thorn bushes straggling across the veld showed the ways of underground watercourses.

Patricia began to worry in case she would not be met. This was something that she had forgotten to arrange with Richard Horton. Would there be anyone? And if not, would she be able to get a taxi? So often in these small places, one had to order a taxi well in advance, especially if one wanted to be met from an early arriving train. If she was met, who would meet her? It would hardly be the delicate Charles Milstead, would it? And surely Mrs Milstead wouldn't be able to leave her baby as well as the three Collins children, unless she left her daughter Antoinette in charge. But wasn't Antoinette at boarding school in Grahamstown? She seemed to remember Richard telling her something like that. But of course, the schools here had a short break in October, before the long drag of the term in the school year.

To Patricia, accustomed to the English scholastic year, which began in the autumn and ended in the summer, it seemed odd to be finishing a school year just before Christmas, and starting the new one shortly after the beginning of the New Year.

The train drew up in a station even smaller than that at Boschfontein. At first, hauling out her suitcase and overnight bag, Patricia, standing on the platform, could only see an African shifting milk cans at the far end of the platform and a station official who could have been the guard, the stationmaster or a porter, scurrying away in the opposite direction. Just as well, she thought, that the conductor had collected her ticket long before they drew into Blouvlei.

She became aware of a tall, handsome woman approaching her, a woman verging on middle-age, whose dark hair, done in a somewhat untidy bun on the nape of her neck, was frosted here and there with silver.

'Miss Lang?' said the woman. 'I'm Maggie van der Berg, Charles Milstead's sister. We thought it would be less overwhelming if I took you to breakfast at our place before letting you be engulfed in children. After all, you do need a bit of a breather after two nights in a train, don't you? Is this all you have with you? Come along, then. Your trunk has arrived all right, and is at Number Five, so that you'll be able to unpack as and when you like.'

Following Mrs van der Berg, who had seized her suitcase in a determined hand, Patricia heard again Richard's voice saying: *His sister's married to one of the two local doctors.*

If Mr and Mrs Milstead were anything like Mrs van der Berg, she thought, then they'd make pleasant neighbours. There had been none of the avid curiosity that she had come to dread, which did not seem to be as dead as she had hoped while she had been immured with old Mrs Hughes. There was only a friendly welcome here.

The Van der Berg home was the only double-storey building in the dorp, save for the two hotels and one of the banks. Patricia ate an enormous breakfast in a pleasant dining-room overlooking a garden with a vine-covered pergola which, in autumn, would be covered with grapes.

Dr van der Berg, like his wife, was pleasantly welcoming and friendly, but without any eager curiosity to see the daughter and stepdaughter of the couple who had been so tragically killed on the eve of the husband's being arrested for embezzlement.

'I'm glad Richard found you,' he said over a plate of bacon and eggs. 'Mary and Charles are very good to the children who love them, but even though they're no longer with a parent, it's good for them to get back to their own home, amid familiar surroundings.'

'But I didn't know the house had been their home,' said Patricia. 'I knew it was Horton property; Mr Horton told me that, but he said that it had been let to a succession of people.'

'Yes, then he gave it to Martha to live in with the children while Graham was in the Antarctic,' said the doctor. 'Their home was well outside Grahamstown—convenient enough for the Varsity with a car, and easy enough to reach the town, but lonely for a woman with three children, the eldest only ten, and no man in the house. Martha knew and liked the Milsteads, so was quite ready to fall in with her brother's plans for her, and to let her own house and go and live next door to them. She let it unfurnished for a year, and brought all her things here. Graham thought it was a lot of wasted effort, for only a year, but Martha said that it was hopeless to let a house furnished for a year. Tenants never look after your things, so she said. I don't know whether she had a presentiment about what was to happen; I don't think so. I think it was simply as she said. She didn't want to leave her beloved household goods to the tender mercies of strangers. I must go, dear.' He turned to his wife. 'Mrs Lottering rang while you were at the station. She says the old man's been taken bad again. I know what that means; that he had a heavy night at the pub last night, and that his ulcer's playing up. The only time that man has the proper food and treatment is when I shove him into the Cottage Hospital, and then half the time he signs his own discharge.'

Reluctantly, he heaved himself to his feet and kissed his wife goodbye, waving to Patricia.

'I'm not saying goodbye to you,' he said. 'I'm sure

we'll meet again soon. I only hope it isn't in the course of duty, but with three children to cope with, one can't count on that!'

On this optimistic note, he left.

'Now, Pat,' said Mrs van der Berg, 'I'm going to call you Pat, and my name's Maggie. It's much more friendly to be on Christian name terms, isn't it? You'll feel less strange. I'm sure you can do with a bit of a rest. I've got one or two chores to be done, and I've got to rush along to the shops. When I get back, we'll have a cup of tea and then I'll run you up to Green Street. By that time you ought to be rested and more able to cope. All right? Don't worry about Mary. I told her last night that I was keeping you for breakfast and then giving you a chance to reorientate yourself after your long train journey. It's more comfortable in here than it is in the dining-room.' She showed Patricia into a comfortable lounge with low chairs and a large bookcase.

'Don't be afraid to put your feet up if you want to,' she said, 'and if you want something to read, help yourself.'

Browsing at the bookcase, Patricia was surprised to find that a large proportion of the books were by her favourite author, Josephine Cantrell. There were all the ones that she had read, and some that she had not. *Winds Across the Sea* she had read in England. *The Faithful Heart* was a fairly recent one; that she had read soon after she had come back to South Africa for good. *Summer Blossoming* must be fairly new; she had not seen that title. She glanced at the title page and saw that it had been published the previous year. She curled up with it in one of the deep armchairs, and soon was so engrossed that she did not hear Maggie van der Berg when she came back into the room.

Maggie laughed. 'I made sure you'd be sound asleep,'

she said. 'I see you found something to read.'

'It's one I haven't read,' said Patricia. 'Mrs—Maggie, do you think I could take it up to Green Street with me and finish it? I'd take great care of it and bring it back safely.'

'But of course!' Maggie, she thought, looked inordinately pleased. 'Now I'm going to call Timnath to get us some tea.'

A tall African maid brought in a tray of tea and set it on the low table before them. Maggie spoke rapidly and at length to her in a language unintelligible to Patricia.

'*Aikona*, missis,' said Timnath.

Maggie spoke some more, and Patricia was fascinated by their long conversation. She had mostly only been in the Western Cape, leaving it only for short holidays at hotels, where the staff, of whatever colour, spoke English.

'Bother,' said Maggie when Timnath had gone. 'That means I shan't see the butcher when he brings the meat, and I wanted to. Well, I'll just have to trust that Timnath's got the message right.'

'What language was that?' asked Patricia.

'Xhosa; they all speak it round here,' said Maggie. 'I forgot you spent most of your childhood in England, didn't you?'

'I went to school there. I do hope the maid at Number Five will be able to speak English. Mr Horton said he'd asked Mrs Milstead to find one.' If they all spoke this incomprehensible language, how was she to get on with them?

There were very few Africans in Capetown. There were the Cape Malays, a very respectable community, Moslems almost without exception, who kept themselves to themselves, and the Cape Coloured community. This group has a little of everyone in their blood. Descend-

43

ants of the now-vanished Hottentots, the original inhabitants of the Cape, they had in their veins an admixture of African, Malay, Indian, and, from various sources in the far distant past, a small leavening of white. They varied from sallow to *café-au-lait* to dark, as dark as the full-blooded Africans. Mostly their hair was frizzy, although that of the women grew longer than the peppercorn fuzz of the African. In some cases, their hair was as straight as that of the Malays.

They were a gay, volatile group of people, with an impish sense of humour and a fund of songs, which they would sing walking along the street, accompanying themselves on a guitar hung from their shoulders. They could speak and understand both English and Afrikaans, though their *lingua franca* was a mixture of the two, known as Kitchen Dutch.

Patricia began to feel that she had entered a new and alien world.

'Don't worry,' said Maggie. 'Most of the Africans round here speak English as well as their own language. A lot of them are trilingual as well, and can speak Afrikaans. I think Mary was going to try and get Minah, the sister of Timnath. She speaks very good English. Now, if you're ready, I'll run you up to Green Street.'

Once more Patricia felt her apprehension creeping back. How would the Milsteads receive her? How much had Richard told them about her? Would they stare at the daughter of Mrs Verity—Garth Verity's stepdaughter—as though they thought she was some specimen escaped from the zoo as the girls in the Horton and Verity offices had done? Possibly not; they would know all about her.

She remembered that Mrs Milstead's first husband had been a Verity, and somewhat unsatisfactory, from what Richard had told her. How would she react to having a Verity by marriage, as it were, thrust down beside

44

her as a next-door neighbour?

They found Mary Milstead sitting placidly darning socks on the back stoep of her home, while two toddlers played and squabbled on a rug inside a playpen beside her. When they appeared, she put down the sock that she had been darning and stood up to welcome them.

'We've dumped Pat's cases in the hall,' said Maggie. 'I thought we'd find you out here.'

'Sit down. What about some tea?' Mary hardly greeted you at all; she just accepted you as one of her company and made as if you had been there all the time.

'Pat and I've only just had a cup,' said Maggie.

Mary gazed at her. 'Go on, Maggie, you're slipping! You can usually manage more than one. You can, can't you, Pat?'

Pat hesitated, and Mary went on, 'I wish you would. Charles hasn't had any yet, and he's been working in the study since eight o'clock. The text of *The Winter Lagoon* is being difficult. Remember, Maggie, that one he did the sketches for when we stayed at Knysna in June that time? He wouldn't even have tea in the study when I took him in a cup, let alone leave the book and come out. Still, he might have come unstuck by now. When I've given Rosie a shout for some tea, I'll yell at him and see what that does.'

She went along to the back door and called, 'Rosie!'

It seemed, thought Pat, that she meant it quite literally when she said that she would 'shout for Rosie.' Pat wondered how it would sound when she 'yelled' at Charles.

'Marriage to Charles has brought Mary out,' murmured Maggie. 'When she first came up here to nurse him and my father, she was such a quiet, subdued little person. Yes, didn't you know? that was how she and Charles met, and I've always been so glad. Charles was more or less in a wheelchair with occasional sorties on crutches when she first came, and his accident put my father back so much that he was almost an invalid from that time on.'

Pat was amused to hear Mary described as a 'little person.' She was as tall as Pat herself—still, Maggie was even taller; she must be at least five foot nine.

They heard a clattering of cups somewhere in the house, and Mary emerged from the back door and walked along the stoep to a wide-open window a few yards from where they were sitting.

'Charles!' she called.

'Oy-oy!'

'How's it going? Coming on better?'

'Not too bad; why?'

'Because Maggie's brought Pat Lang up and . . .'

'Pat Lang?'

'Don't be obtuse, darling. Pat's the girl Richard found, who was actually willing to bury herself in Blouvlei and look after Martha's children.'

'Of course. Sorry, love; I'm not yet quite with you.'

Mary laughed. 'So I noticed. Well, any minute there'll be tea on the stoep.'

A fairish, untidy head poked out of the window.

'Now that I do call epoch-making,' it said. 'I thought if I emerged and demanded tea now, I'd get told that it was too near lunch time. Maggie, Pat—I may call you Pat, mayn't I?—between you, you've performed a miracle. You've induced Mary to produce tea when lunch is almost due to appear.'

'You're just being awkward, darling,' said Mary placidly, sitting down again as her husband disappeared from his window and reappeared at the back door at the same time that Rosie appeared with a tray of tea-things. 'It's barely twelve, and you know we never start lunch until well after one.'

46

She gazed down at the two toddlers in the playpen, who appeared to be identically clad, and inextricably mixed.

'This one's yours,' she said, grabbing a bare, fat ankle. 'No, this one is.'

'It's a wise mother that knows her own child,' Charles grinned wickedly.

'It's easy,' said his wife. 'Look at this. Podge!' she shouted. Immediately the tangle of fat arms and legs resolved itself into two chubby toddlers, pink-cheeked and fair-haired. One of them stood up and staggered on unsteady legs to the side of the playpen, where he held up his arms to be picked up.

'It never fails,' said Mary. 'You pick him up, Pat. If he gets used to you while he's with us whom he knows, he's less likely to get a sudden fright at being with a stranger when you get him next door.'

Patricia picked up the adorable bundle.

'That's Auntie Pat,' said Mary.

'Cat,' said Podge, pulling Patricia's hair.

'No, darling, not Cat, Pat,' said Mary. '*Auntie* Pat.'

'Pad-pad! Pod-pod! *Padda, padda!*' gurgled Podge delightedly.

'And *Padda*, in case you didn't know,' said Mary, 'is the Afrikaans word for a frog!' She sighed. 'It's no good. I can never get any of the children to call anyone "Aunt". Even my daughter Toinette weighed straight in and called Charles by his christian name the first time she met him, when she was about fourteen, and the idea of getting married hadn't entered our heads.'

'Where is Toinette?' asked Maggie.

'Taken Peggy and David into the dorp for ice-creams,' replied Toinette's mother. 'I hope she doesn't fill them so full that they're sick or spoil their dinner. Sometimes she hasn't the sense that she was born with.'

47

'Nonsense,' said Charles. 'You know she's as bright as they come, and you're as proud as Punch of her, only you won't admit it.'

'I daren't admit it. She might sense it and get a swelled head. You spoil her enough. I suppose it's no good asking you to stay and have lunch with us, Maggie?'

Maggie rose. 'I'm afraid not, my dear. I ought to be getting back now to get it for Paul. If I see the children, I'll tell them to get a move on, shall I?'

She kissed Mary, pulled a rude face at her brother and then kissed Patricia. 'You just come and see Paul and me sometimes, when the babes get too much for you,' she said. 'Get Mary to bring you, and find a joint baby-sitter for both lots.'

Patricia felt quite lost when she had gone.

At lunch, Patricia had the opportunity to observe her new charges without them realising that they were under scrutiny. Peggy, the eldest, was fair, and had a rather prim look until one realised that she was merely shy in the presence of a stranger. David was a rough little boy with perpetually skinned knees. Both he and his sister called Mary and Charles by their Christian names. Podge, beginning to talk, tried. Whenever he looked across the table to Patricia, he would chortle with delight, and shout, 'Padda! Padda!'

When the meal was over, after a short break, Mary suggested that they should move over to Number Five, the house next door which the young Collins family knew as home. Thanks to Mary's cheerful but not over-sympathetic mothering since they had lost their own parents, they had settled down so well in the house next door to their own that they were rather dubious about moving back next door, and with a stranger at that. Peggy clung rather closely to Mary, and David hung back at the garden gate.

'Come on,' said Mary. 'Peggy, don't you want to get back to the pictures on your bedroom wall? David, won't it be nice to be able to have your trains out again?' She turned to Patricia. 'He's got a set of electric trains set out in the spare room next to his bedroom. You ought to see it; it's really good for a boy of six, especially as he's put it up with very little help, except that Martha got a carpenter to put up trestle tables round the room so that the lines could run round on them.'

The only one of the three about whom Patricia felt happy was the baby, Podge, who had attached himself to her. She was carrying him now, while Peggy took her overnight case, and Mary her suitcase. He was becoming heavier by the minute, but she was grateful for his freely-offered friendship. She was once more beginning to feel a little forlorn and apprehensive at the thought of being left alone in sole charge of three perfectly strange children. Mary, evidently sensing how she felt, said, 'David and Peg, take Pat's cases to her room. We'll go and put Podge in his playpen; he won't rest yet. He's too excited at all the changes. It's all right, Pat, it's all ready for him with his toys in it.'

She led the way to a large dining-room, one end of which was filled by the dining table, and at the other end of which was a playpen on a rug, strewn with stuffed toys and rag dolls, most of which were a little the worse for wear.

'Put him down,' she said. Podge clung.

'Put him down, Pat,' said Mary again. 'If you're not firm now, you'll be making a stick for your own back. You can't possibly cart that great lump round all the time, and the quicker he finds it out, the better for you and for him.'

Hardening her heart, Patricia firmly deposited her warm, cuddlesome burden in his playpen. At once he opened his mouth, took a deep breath and started to

49

roar. Mary grabbed Patricia's arm in time to prevent her from picking him up again.

'Leave him,' she said. 'He'll stop it as soon as he knows we're not taking any notice of him.'

She drove Patricia out of the room before her. 'Now, this will be your room. All right?'

Patricia gazed round, entranced. It was a lovely room. The walls were distempered cream, and on them were reproductions of paintings by South African artists —all landscapes. There was one of Table Mountain, looking across a tumbling expanse of the Atlantic from Blaawberg Strand. Another showed the rolling hills of an Eastern Cape scene, with a candelabrum aloe in flame-coloured bloom in the foreground. One over the bed was of the mountains in the Western Cape—somewhere near Paarl or Wellington, at a guess, thought Patricia. The rocky kranzes at the summit were an incredible shade, a mixture of pink, orange and palest mauve all in one subtle blend.

'I never believed that colour when I saw it in pictures,' said Patricia. 'Only when Garth had to go to Ceres on business and took Mummy and me, and we arrived in the evening, then I saw those mountains in the sunset and knew that the pictures were true.'

The furniture, as well as being more than adequate, was beautiful.

'Isn't this stinkwood?' asked Patricia, running her hand down a roomy wardrobe in a gleaming, satiny wood.

'Yes. Gavin's father had a plantation near Knysna. A lot of their furniture was stinkwood.'

The chest of drawers matched the wardrobe, and the dressing table was in the Dolly Varden style, the curtain round matching those at the window and the bedspread, a green leafy design on a pale fawn ground.

'Do you want a quick wash?' asked Mary. 'I'll go

and make us a cup of tea. Yes, the larder's stocked; I saw to that. Good grief, you don't think we expected you to come and take over and have to shop for essentials right away, did you? All right, you freshen up while I make the tea. By that time, the kids'll have made the acquaintance of their old treasures again, and there's a cake, an iced one. That'll finish the welcome home process satisfactorily.'

Patricia did not think she was very long, but when she went into the dining-room, tea was on the table, Mary was pouring out, and Peggy and David were tucking into enormous slices of iced cake, talking nineteen to the dozen as they did so. Only when she looked down to see how Podge was faring did Patricia realise that he must have stopped crying some time ago. He was sitting quiet, absorbed in a large red gingham-covered toy frog. The look on his face was angelic.

' Padda. Padda,' he repeated softly and raptly, over and over again.

' I'm afraid you'll be a frog for the rest of your time here, Pat,' said Mary, handing her a cup of tea. ' It's a compliment really. That ghastly red check frog's his favourite toy, and if he's associated you with it, your troubles are over as far as he's concerned.'

Peggy raised innocent eyes from her cake.

' That's a good name for you, Pat,' she said. ' We'll call you " Frog ".'

David appeared to find this exquisitely funny. ' Frog, Pat the Frog!' He rolled about in his chair in ecstasies of mirth.

' That'll do, David!' Mary's voice was stern, but there was a twinkle in her eyes.

' At any rate,' she murmured under cover of the noise being made by the children, ' if they've given you a nickname, you shouldn't find it too hard going. They'll play jokes on you, but there'll be no malice and they'll do what they're told if you remember to be firm. You're on the way to having arrived!'

Patricia managed a smile, but there was a prickling sensation behind her eyes and deep thankfulness in her heart. If the children accepted her and learned to love her, she might manage to do this job really well. It was important that she should; important to the children and to Richard Horton, their uncle and guardian, and important to Patricia's self-respect.

CHAPTER IV

She would unpack as much as she could when the children were in bed, thought Patricia. It was no sort of use trying to do it with them possibly needing her all the time. In this she was wrong. Soon after Mary had left, Peggy and David disappeared to the bottom of the garden where, from what she could see from the back stoep, they appeared to be playing quite happily. Podge had dropped off to sleep in his playpen, and although Patricia wondered if she ought to wake him—might he not be wakeful tonight if he slept too long now?—she remembered her young aunt's toddler in England, who became fretful and overtired if he missed his afternoon rest, and was even more difficult to settle to sleep at night.

With the house quiet, she had finished her unpacking in little over half an hour. She dragged her trunk out into the passage. Mary had said that the maid would come in the morning. She could help move the trunk to somewhere more suitable. Patricia decided that she would explore in the morning. Possibly there was a boxroom somewhere at the back of the house. There were one or two doors off the back stoep that she hadn't yet investigated.

Podge was still asleep, and the other two were still playing in the garden. Patricia looked at her watch. An early supper would be a good idea, and she was dog-tired and could do with an early night herself.

There were plenty of eggs and plenty of milk and butter, so she made tea and toast and a large plate of scrambled eggs. Podge was still sound asleep in his playpen. She would put him to bed when they had finished supper. If he woke and clamoured for attention before then, it was just too bad. Tomorrow she would work out a routine; tonight she must just play it by ear.

The children, she decided, could bath while she did the washing up, and then she would be free to bathe Podge and give him his bottle.

'He was off all-night feeds,' Mary had told her, 'but although he was too young to know what had happened, he was old enough to miss his mother and to be upset by change, even if it was just coming to stay next door with us whom he knew well enough. I found that he was all right during the daytime, but the only way I could settle him at night was to give him a bottle. He's very good; doesn't take long. I suppose it's just that extra bit of human contact—T.L.C., as we say in hospital.'

'T.L.C.—' Patricia had looked enquiringly at Mary.

Mary laughed. 'Tender loving care,' she had answered. 'For years now, doctors have realised more and more that love and affection do as much for people as medicines, especially for children.'

She put the meal on the table, and found that when she went to call Peggy and David, they had come up from the garden and were playing about on the back stoep with much giggling. Well, they seemed happy enough, she thought, with a sigh of relief.

'Supper's on the table,' she said.

She was surprised when the two children waited before starting.

'We haven't said grace,' Peggy reminded her solemnly.

Patricia had never been taught to say grace at home. The only time that she had said grace before meals was when she had had lunch at school, when an assistant mistress had barked: 'For what we are about to receive, may the Lord make us truly thankful,' as though she

54

personally would have something to say about it if He didn't.

'All right,' she said. 'Go ahead and say it.'

'Which one shall we say?' asked David.

'*Thank you for the world . . .*'

'No, I don't like that one. *For these and all His Mercies . . .*'

'No, *For this and every plateful . . .*'

'No, that's a soppy one. All right, we'll have *For these.*'

Both children closed their eyes and folded their hands. Either of them, thought Patricia, could have served as a model for 'The Littlest Angel', only that was Podge. In perfect unison, they recited: *For these and all His Mercies, may God's Holy Name be praised.*

Then four blue eyes shot open and two noisy, healthy children clamoured for supper.

In an incredibly short time, the table was clear, every plate polished almost as clean as though it had already been washed.

'D'you want us to help clear away?' asked Peggy.

'Well, you could help carry the things into the kitchen,' said Patricia. 'I'll wash up, though, while you two bath. You needn't get straight into bed, though, as long as you don't hang about too long. Or you could get into bed and read if you like. Thing is, if I'm getting clear while you two are in the bathroom, I'll be able to wake Podge and take my time about getting him clean and ready for bed afterwards. Tomorrow we'll work out a routine that suits the lot of us, but tonight we'll just have to get done what needs doing. All right?'

Two angelic children nodded. Two voices in unison said 'Fine.' Peggy, who evidently was not as prim as she sometimes appeared, added *sotto voce*, 'Frog.'

Pat laughed. 'All right, off with you!'

. . . . .

The washing-up done, the children quiet if not asleep, and Podge put down in a contented milky daze, Patricia decided that she could relax. She soaked in a bath and, feeling much better, went to the kitchen to heat herself a glass of milk to take to bed. On her way back to her room, she glanced into the two small adjoining rooms in which Peggy and David slept. Both appeared to be asleep, but Patricia did not like to shine the torch which she had found in the hall on them in case, if they were asleep, she might wake them, and if not, she might start something that she could not control. She was too tired to have to cope with mischief tonight.

Podge, his cot in a room which had a communicating door into hers, which she left open, was sleeping the deep sleep of contented babyhood, bottom in air. With a sigh of relief, Patricia turned on the bedside lamp, switched off the top light, and taking off her dressing-gown, climbed wearily into bed.

It was when she stretched out her feet that she became aware of something amiss, something that moved in her bed. With a smothered gasp, she leapt out of bed and then, gingerly, she drew back the bedclothes. There, sitting blinking at her from the middle of the bed, was a large, warty toad. She let her breath out in a long sigh.

'Hello, old fellow,' she said softly. 'How on earth did you get there, and where's your proper home?'

A smothered giggle from the hall outside answered the first part of the question. Of course, the children were taking a rise out of her. Children always tried to take a rise out of someone new who was put in charge. Her entire future with the Collins children depended upon how she handled this. She turned to the seemingly empty doorway.

'Are you two there?' she called in a light, gay voice. 'Just come and see what I've found!'

56

Two figures in dressing gowns and bedroom slippers crept in. Patricia stood gazing in admiration at her unexpected guest.

' Isn't he handsome?' she asked them.

' D'you—d'you really like him?' asked Peggy.

' Of course!' This was true. Patricia had always had a weakness for the odd animals that could be found in the garden. Seldom had she seen such a fine specimen as this one, but most of her garden ramblings had been when she was at school in England. Her mother and stepfather had usually lived in luxury flats, and in any case, when she was staying with them, they were usually on holiday in a hotel.

' I think he's fine,' she said to the children. ' Don't you?'

' *We* like him,' said Peggy, ' but we didn't think you would.'

' We thought you'd be frightened,' added David.

Patricia ignored this. If they did not realise that they had given themselves away, she would leave it that way.

' I wish I knew where he lived,' she said musingly. ' Toads don't really like being indoors. I'll have to take him back into the garden, but if I knew just where he lived, it would save him having to find his way home.'

' I know where he lives,' volunteered David.

' You do? That's good. Where is it?'

' Down at the bottom of the garden by that old shed.'

' Well, I see you've both got good stout bedroom slippers and dressing gowns. One of you bring the torch and light the way.'

Swiftly and gently, Patricia picked up the toad in both hands, hoping that he would not jump out and necessitate a search all over the house. He was either content to be where he was, or so shocked with what he had been through that night as to be unable to move, for he lay quiescent, pulsating slightly in Patricia's cupped hands. Both Peggy and David came with her to the bottom of the garden, Peggy holding the torch to light the way, and David to see that his friend the toad was put in his rightful place.

'What'll you do if he jumps before we get there?' he asked when they were half way down the path. 'Look for him to take him home?'

Patricia laughed. 'I certainly shall not!' she exclaimed. 'We'd never find him. He'd hide straight away. No, he'd probably find his way home, but I think it's better if we can to put him where he's usually found. That's where he likes to be.'

'There!' David pointed to the long grass in which stood one or two dilapidated outhouses, one which had seemingly been an outside bedroom at some time, a potting shed and an outside toilet.

'He lives under the potting shed,' said David.

'I'm not going into that long grass in my dressing gown,' said Patricia, 'nor are you. The grass is probably soaking wet with dew.'

Stooping, she let the toad go, and after blinking at them dazedly for a few seconds in the light of the powerful torch, he hopped rapidly through the long grass until he disappeared beneath the wooden buildings.

'Now,' said Patricia briskly, 'bed. I'm tired if you're not. I heated myself some milk, but I suppose it's got cold by now. I'll heat us all some more. It's not really so warm outside at this hour of night, and we don't want you catching colds.'

'We always have warm milk when we go to bed,' said Peggy, skipping up the path beside Patricia.

'Why didn't you tell me? Of course you shall have it every night, then. You know, you'll have to help me, Peggy. There's lots I don't know.'

'All right, I'll let you know if there's anything we

usually do that you don't, and if there's anything we don't do that you do, won't we, David?'

There was a grunt from behind them. David, with the torch, had stopped to examine a stick insect that was clinging to the hedge.

'That'll be a great help,' said Patricia. 'I don't guarantee always to follow your instructions, but it's a help to know what's usually done, isn't it? Come on, Dave; you'll catch cold, and we need the torch to see our way up the steps.'

David came running.

'Now,' said Patricia when they were all inside and the back door locked once more, 'you two get to bed and I'll bring your milk to you.' Already she had the pan on one of the hotplates of the Aga.

The two showed signs of wanting to keep her talking when she took their milk along, but she scotched this; she was far too tired. She only waited while they drank their milk and then tucked them up. David was almost asleep as she pulled the sheets round him. Peggy, in the next room, was drowsy. Patricia tucked her in, picked up the empty glass and turned the light out. As she reached the door, a drowsy little voice reached her.

'I do like you, Frog,' it said.

When her alarm went off at seven the next morning, Patricia was tempted to turn over and go to sleep again. A long train journey and then the strain of meeting new people who, she had been sure, would disapprove of her, as well as worrying about how she would get on with the children, had worn her out. She had been thankful, when she finally tumbled into bed, that her fears had been groundless, but still bone-weary. Too weary to get to sleep right away. For the first time since she had met the children, in the darkness of her bedroom,

59

she had time to remember Richard Horton. She must succeed, she told herself fiercely. She just must! Against his better judgement, he had played a hunch when he employed her to look after his dead sister's children. Somehow it was desperately important that he should have done the right thing—more important than merely being her job which she did not want to lose. In an odd way, it was the most important thing in her life just now; a challenge, and . . . something more than a challenge.

She went to sleep and dreamed that she and Richard Horton were looking for a toad by the light of a hurricane lamp, in the long grass by the little wooden buildings at the bottom of the garden, and when the alarm clock sounded at seven o'clock, she felt as though she had been asleep for about five minutes, but she had to get up and unlock the door to let in the maid who Mary told her would arrive at that time.

Dragging on her dressing gown, and thrusting her feet into her slippers, she stumbled to the back door. The maid was already there, a very black, very thin African woman wearing a high black felt turban, a black shawl and a long dark blue, white-sprigged skirt. Round her hips as a kind of basque was tied a gaily striped bath towel, and round her waist she had tied a white apron. When Patricia opened the door, she stood up from the back doorstep where she had been patiently waiting.

' Good morning, madam,' she said in a deep voice, very different from the quick, light, high voices of the *volkies* in Capetown.

' Good morning. What's your name?' Patricia endeavoured to wake up sufficiently to treat the woman with courtesy.

' Angelina, madam. I used to work for the other madam.'

' The other—you mean Mrs Collins, the children's

mother?'

'Yes, madam. I work for the other madam all the time she is here.'

That, thought Patricia, wasn't so long; only about a year before she and her husband were killed. Well, the main thing is that we keep the children happy.

'Well, Angelina,' she said, 'come in. You'd better start by getting breakfast. It had better be boiled eggs this morning; they're easy. I put out the eggs last night.'

'Good, madam. I will cook the breakfast.'

She moved over to the stove and Patricia, thankful that Mary Milstead had found the maid who had worked for Mrs Collins so that she did not need to be shown where everything was, went to wake the children and get dressed herself.

The two elder childen were very quiet at first, at the breakfast table, then, 'Are you going to tell Uncle Dick about the toad?' asked Peggy.

It took Patricia a few seconds to work out that Uncle Dick was none other than Richard Horton.

'I hadn't thought about it. Why?'

'We'd be grateful if you didn't. He'd be cross with us.'

'Cross with you?' Why? Surely Richard Horton had a sense of humour? she thought. She had caught glimmerings of it. It would have to be a very humourless person who would take a prank like that seriously.

'Well, he told us—David and me—that we'd have to come back to our old house because Mary couldn't be expected to have us all the time. You see, Uncle Charles has a bad leg, although he can walk on it very well now, but a few years ago, he had to sit in a wheel chair all the time, and then he had to walk with crutches. Even now, when he has to walk far he takes a walking stick.

'Well, Uncle Dick said that he'd have to get someone to look after us—a lady. He's too busy—besides, a man can't look after babies and girls like a lady can. So he told us we must be good and not do anything to make the lady go away. We didn't know he'd get anyone young like you. We thought it would be someone like Mrs Browning.'

'Who's Mrs Browning?' asked Patricia.

'The Matron at the hostel of the girls' school,' said Peggy in disgust. 'She's fat and silly and she calls all the girls little dears, even the girls in Standard Ten. We were having fits at first, because we thought Uncle Dick might send us as boarders. It wouldn't be so bad for David; the Matron at the junior boys' hostel is quite nice. But I couldn't stand living in the hostel all the term with that stupid Mrs Browning.'

Patricia was silent for a moment, in thought. Mary Milstead had said that she simply could not persuade any of the children to call adults 'Aunt' or 'Uncle'. It seemed that the exception to this rule was Richard Horton. Well, she could understand that. He had it in him to command awe, even in such disrespectful youngsters as the two elder Collins children.

'Do you like your Uncle Dick?' she asked on impulse, knowing as she spoke that it was hardly a wise question.

'Ooh, yes!' Both children were sure of this.

'He's simply fantabulous!' said Peggy.

'He helps me with my trains when he comes,' added David.

'And he always takes us to have ice-creams at the café.'

'And he drives us out to Andrew and Erica's farm.'

'Where's that?' asked Patricia, 'and who are Andrew and Erica?'

From their somewhat involved explanations, it seemed that Andrew and Erica were a Mr and Mrs Scott who had a farm called Applegarth, somewhere up in the mountains, a little way towards the coast.

'At night, if it's clear,' said Peggy, ' you can see the lights of Aloe Bay from the front stoep.'

'And Andrew lets me play with baby goats.' This was David.

'He breeds goats for mohair,' said Peggy with a knowledgeable air, then, with a rapid descent into little girlhood—'they're *sweet*! The babies, I mean, not the grown-up goats. We're not allowed to go near those; they might butt.'

'May we be excused?' asked David, suddenly tired of the conversation.

'Of course. What are you going to do?' Then, seeing a look of reserve come down over their faces, and remembering how she had hated being questioned about her doings as a child, Patricia hastily added, 'because I thought that later on, when our breakfast has been digested a little, we could put Podge into his pushcart and go into the dorp for ice-cream.'

'*Oh, groovy!*' and: 'Darling Frog, how fab!' exclaimed David and Peggy simultaneously and respectively. They tore out, and as they were heard rushing screaming excitedly down the garden, Toinette Verity put her head round the door.

'Am I intruding?' she asked. ' Mom sent me round to see if you were managing all right, or if there was anything we could do.'

'We're managing fine so far,' said Patricia, ' but sit down and have a cup of tea. There's still plenty.'

Toinette slid into the chair just vacated by Peggy. 'I won't say no,' she agreed.

Patricia studied her surreptitiously as she drank her tea. She was a very pretty girl, with soft, wavy brown hair drawn back into a pony-tail, bright brown eyes and a glowing complexion. She was tall and still at the leggy stage, but later on, when she settled down, she would probably be very lovely indeed.

She must have been about fourteen when her mother married Charles Milstead, thought Patricia, and yet she seemed to be on far easier terms than she—Patricia—had ever been with her own stepfather. It could be that although she was at boarding school, she only had a little over a hundred miles to travel, and could reach home and be reached easily if necessary. Patricia had, since her mother's remarriage, always seemed to be a visitor in her home, although she was officially a citizen of the country, because of the long stretches of time that she had spent at school so far away.

'Had any trouble with the kids?' asked Toinette. 'We had an idea that they were plotting something, but we couldn't find out what it was, so Mom thought it better not to warn you, because if we were wrong, or if it fell flat, you'd only be worrying and making an atmosphere.'

Pat giggled. 'Not what you could really call trouble,' she said. 'I promised not to tell "Uncle Dick." So there *is* someone who they're in awe of enough to call him "Uncle"?'

'Oh yes, everyone else but Dick Horton is on a level with them, everyone who's known by their parents by their christian names, that is. Teachers and people who are only rather formal acquaintances get the "Mr, Mrs, and Miss" treatment, but don't think you'll ever be anything but "Pat" to them,' said Toinette.

'That's just where you're wrong!' Patricia giggled again. 'Already I'm "Frog" to Peggy.'

'"Frog"? Oh, because of Podge's "Padda"?'

'Partly. Partly, I think, because they put a toad in my bed last night.'

Toinette's eyes were wide with amusement and something like horror. 'They *didn't*? So *that* was what the

64

little devils were plotting. What did you do?'

' Well, I was going to take him out into the garden when I discovered that they were hiding behind my bedroom door giggling, so I got one of them to bring the torch and show me where he lives.'

' You mean *you* picked him up?'

' Why not?'

' Well, this is one of their favourite ploys. They both adore anything alive in the garden. We've had to be dreadfully stern about snakes or they'd make friends with them too. But one day when Mom was giving a rather stuffy tea-party, they frightened most of the old lady guests into fits by bringing in a branch with a simply enormous chameleon clinging to it.'

' Good for them!' exclaimed Patricia.

' That's what I thought; so did Charles, but as Mom pointed out, one has to draw the line somewhere.'

' They made me promise not to tell Uncle Dick, as he'd be furious with them.'

' I'll bet he would. He tried to get them to promise that they'd be nice to you.'

' Well, so they have.'

' Most people wouldn't have thought that putting a toad in your bed your first night was very nice.'

' Oh, that was just to try me out to find out if I was human or not. Of course, I'll have to persuade them that it isn't always a good thing. I mean, I'm young and can take it, but if it was someone old with a bad heart, they could have been frightened half to death when they felt the poor toad moving at their feet.'

' I'd have screamed the place down,' admitted Toinette.

' I nearly did myself, then I realised that it was probably some trick of the kids and got out quick to see what they'd landed me with. I'll also have to get it into their heads that cold-blooded animals like frogs, toads and lizards don't like being held in hot human hands.'

Toinette looked at Patricia with respect. 'You're going to have your work cut out,' she said.

Patricia laughed. 'Apparently they were scared stiff that Mr Horton was going to get someone like Mrs Browning to look after them,' she said.

'So were we. At first his idea was someone middle-aged, responsible and motherly. Martha was nearly thirty when she died, but she was still young and gay —a wonderful person. They'd have been miserable with someone middle-aged with no sense of humour. We were never more relieved in our lives when you pitched up.'

'Even knowing who I am? Knowing how Mr Horton found me?'

'You mean your being Garth Verity's stepdaughter? What's that got to do with it? Actually, I think the firm, or at any rate, the family, owe you something. You must have been left in an awful predicament. And after all, it wasn't your fault. I don't see how anyone could possibly blame you. And no one could drag in heredity, could they? You were his stepdaughter; no blood relation.'

'Mr Horton nearly dragged in environment,' said Patricia a little wryly. 'Did your mother and stepfather know how he discovered me?'

'We-ell, I did hear a little,' admitted Toinette cautiously. 'Didn't you get caught up in one of Simon's daft schemes?'

' "Caught up" is making it sound much too involuntary,' said Patricia. 'I let myself be caught up in it deliberately.' She gave Toinette a brief but concise outline of the events that had led up to her first meeting with Richard Horton, from her meeting with old Mrs Hughes in the nursing home until her visit to the offices of Horton and Verity, when Richard had admitted that sometimes against his better judgement, he played his hunches.

'That's like Dick Horton,' said Toinette. 'Simon thinks he's a stuffed shirt, and I admit that sometimes he acts like one, but he's a decent sort really. I think it's just because he's a very reserved type. Mom and my Aunt Maggie say he ought to get married. Look, Angelina's hovering to clear the table. I ought to be moving. Look, can I come back at eleven and join you and the imps for your trip to the café for ice-creams?'

'I'd love you to!' It had occurred to Patricia that although Toinette Verity was still in her last term at school and was not yet eighteen, she was nearer in age to Patricia herself than either of the other two women who had befriended her in Blouvlei. Maggie van der Berg must be nearly fifty, and Mary Milstead well over forty. In this, her estimate was slightly wrong. Maggie van der Berg was fifty-four, and Mary just forty.

As Patricia went about tidying the children's rooms and her own, checking the belongings that she had so hastily unpacked the evening before, and supervising the storage of her trunk, as she was checking the stores in the larder and asking Angelina if there was anything special that she needed or had run out of, the thought of Richard Horton was very much in her mind.

So the children were in awe of him, were they? And yet they were, it seemed, very fond of him. It seemed that affection and admiration were not ruled out by wholesome awe.

She wondered if he would ever come to approve of her —really approve, not just take a chance on her being suitable under the kindly supervision of Mary Milstead, because he believed in playing his hunches, even with his own flesh and blood. She hoped so. Somehow, his approval was very important to her.

· · · · ·

Patricia might not have worried so much about Richard Horton's opinion of her had she been able to read the letter that Mary Milstead wrote to him that evening.

Unknown to Patricia, he had indeed asked the Milsteads to keep an eye on things next door, and had asked Mary to drop him a line to let him know how things were turning out with his dubious protegée at the helm.

Toinette, when she had gone home after her early-morning chat with Patricia, had told her mother in confidence about the incident with the toad. 'But she doesn't want it broadcast, as she's afraid that if Dick knows, he'll take reprisals on the children. It seems that he put the fear of God into them to be nice to their new housekeeper, and they imagined someone like that ghastly Mrs Browning! Well, obviously Pat's not like that, but they still put the poor toad in her bed!'

That evening, when Toinette was out with some friends and her husband was busy with his latest manuscript, Mary sat down to write to Richard Horton:

I don't think you need worry about Pat Lang, she wrote. *The kids took to her straight away, and call her 'Frog,' because Podge saw a likeness between her name and that ghastly red gingham toy he calls 'Padda', so to him, she promptly became Padda, translated at once by Peggy into 'Frog,' which, I think, touched and delighted her.*

Toinette and I had an idea they were planning some trick, but although we kept our eyes and ears open, couldn't find out what it was, and held thumbs that it wouldn't be anything too awful. Poor Pat found out, as soon as she got into bed that night. They'd caught a toad—a large one—that lives in the long grass by those derelict outhouses at the end of the garden.

Pat took it all quite calmly. She inspanned one of

*them to bring the torch to show her the way—of course
the little wretches were hiding outside giggling, waiting
for her to scream—and she picked up the toad, and with
David in pyjamas and dressing-gown lighting the way
with the big torch, they went down and put the poor
beast back where it belonged. She told Toinette in
confidence when T. went over this morning to see how
they were getting on. She doesn't want you told in case
there are reprisals—on the children, not on her.*

*I don't fancy she'll have much more trouble with
them, and anyway, school opens next week, so they
won't be underfoot so much . . .*

*By the way, I think we ought to have that long grass
cleared away. The kids won't like it, and toads are
pleasant enough people, but there could be snakes
there . . .*

A few evenings later, sitting in his comfortable bachelor
flat overlooking the sea at Southcliff, Richard Horton
laughed as he read the letter. It seemed that in spite
of misgivings, he had not been mistaken in employing
Patricia Lang to look after his niece and nephews. Mary
had mentioned that Charles approved too, and he had a
high opinion of Charles Milstead's judgement. There
was also a letter from Maggie van der Berg in his mail.
Maggie wrote to let him know that Patricia had arrived
safely, and what a nice child she was. Her husband
Paul, too, was taken with Patricia.

Well, well, he thought. If it had been one of them
or even two, he might have suspected that Patricia had
pulled an act—put on the charm. But for both couples—
Maggie and Paul, Charles and Mary—to like the girl
was good. They couldn't all be wrong. And apparently
she was striking up a friendship with young Toinette.
Toinette was only a schoolgirl, but it was as hard to pull
the wool over her eyes as it was over her stepfather's.

It looked as though the kids were all right for the

time being, he thought, puffing at his pipe and gazing out to sea. It couldn't last, of course. The girl would either get tired of being buried in the country, or fall in love and want to leave to get married. Oh well, sufficient unto the day . . .

The next idea that came into his head had him sitting up in horrified amazement. Utterly ridiculous. She was *far* too young for him!

CHAPTER V

When the children went back to school, Patricia managed to evolve some sort of a routine. She enjoyed the life far more than she had thought she would, in fact once or twice, when she remembered to stop and think, she realised that she was really happy—happier than she had been for a long time. She did not know how long this job was going on, but she realised that she had fallen on her feet.

How many girls with as few qualifications as she had were in a post with everything found including a roof over their heads, good pay and work that they enjoyed? For, she realised, she did enjoy looking after the three Collins children. She missed Antoinette from next door now that that young lady had gone back to boarding school in Grahamstown, but Antoinette wrote as often as she could, amusing letters with neat character sketches of some of her teachers, and said that she looked forward to seeing Patricia when she came home for Christmas.

At first, the silence worried Patricia a little. At night, especially, when she was in bed, when she put down her book and turned out the light, the silence would come rushing in on her and sleep would recede.

Green Street was on the outskirts of the dorp. No car passed; there was seldom any sound from the other houses. All that Patricia could hear as she lay in the darkness was an occasional dog barking in the distance and the chirping of the crickets. It was so very different from the flat in which she had lived with her mother and stepfather, where the sounds of traffic would rumble on and off nearly all night, or the hotel rooms that she had inhabited when she had been looking after Mrs Hughes. It was an even greater contrast to the room not far from the front of the hotel where she had lived when she had gone through the pretence of being engaged to Simon Verity, where she could hear cars leaving the car park until after midnight, on the rare occasions when she went early to bed herself.

The only nights that she had known that were as quiet as this, at least since babyhood, were those that she spent in her grandmother's home, when she was at school in Cheltenham, but even there, although it was every bit as quiet as this, there was a different feel about the night. Although it was a quiet suburb, it was part of a town. You could sense the houses all round—the little new houses on either side, the road leading down to the main road through the town, where, occasionally, a late car would hum through the night. You knew that the station was not far away, and if you were wakeful, could hear an occasional train rumbling through to Gloucester, or up to Birmingham and the north.

Here, all that there was was a huddle of houses, most of them a little way away—Green Street was quite a way from the centre of Blouvlei—and behind the house, the limitless veld, stretching away to the mountains. Patricia's bedroom faced the garden, and beyond the garden was nothing—nothing but veld. As well as silence, there was a vast feeling of emptiness.

In time, however, she came to appreciate the stillness, to relax, and rest. Tired after keeping house and looking after the children, she would drop off to sleep almost as soon as her head touched the pillow.

The one aspect of her new life that Patricia did not like was the early rising that was necessary if she was to get the children off to school in time. She would set her alarm for six o'clock, roll over and doze again until ten or a quarter past, and then go into the kitchen and make herself a cup of tea. Then she would wake Podge, pot him and give him a cup of milk. It was only at night when he was going to sleep that he still had a bottle. Then, leaving him playing peacefully in his cot, she would have a shower or a quick bath and when she was dressed, wake Peggy and David.

By the time that Angelina arrived at seven, the big kettle would be on the hotplate of the Aga, the coals raked, and Patricia would be chivvying the two older children to be dressed and ready for breakfast.

Sometimes, her newly acquired sense of responsibility surprised Patricia herself. One day, when Mary Milstead had brought her baby to play with Podge while she and Patricia enjoyed a quiet cup of tea and a chat on the back stoep, she allowed herself a good grumble about the early mornings.

'Trouble is,' she said, 'I'm hopeless myself in the early mornings, but I daren't let the little wretches know I sympathise with them. And as well as having to get them awake, out of bed and dressed, there's always something mislaid—an arithmetic book or a tennis racquet or something that they simply *must* have today. And I don't care what happens, they must have a decent breakfast before they go to school. I'd rather keep them home than let them go to school empty.'

Mary agreed heartily, and Patricia was silent for a few moments, silenced by surprise at the fact that in her own voice and sentiments, she had caught an echo of her English grandmother. Old Mrs Lang was the last person with whom Patricia would have expected to find herself agreeing. She had loved the old lady, but had been in awe of her. There had been little overt affection between them, but she had been sorry, when her school-days were over, that they would meet so seldom. Mrs Lang had died in her sleep just in time to save her from hearing the news of her daughter-in-law's tragedy. Patricia had felt it very little, sorrow for her grandmother's death being swallowed up in the greater, more immediate tragedy. Now that her life was more regular and peaceful, she sometimes found time to think about the old days when she was at school in England, and to wonder how things would have turned out had her grandmother lived.

Granny, she supposed, would have paid her fare back, and would have launched her in life in Cheltenham in whatever unskilled job she could find that was suitable. She wondered if she would have been happier than she was now, and said as much to Mary.

'You once said you had a young aunt over there,' said Mary. 'The one whose babies you used to help with. I'm surprised she didn't send for you. After all, she's your only remaining relative—you can't count the odd Verity connection. They're no relation. You owe them nothing and they've no responsibility towards you.'

'Aunt Gwennie couldn't afford to pay my passage over,' said Patricia. 'I suppose the estate might just have stretched far enough to squeeze a tourist class passage out of the débris, but it never occurred to me to ask. I was too shattered at the time, and then old Mrs Hughes—your late mother-in-law—turned up.'

Mary laughed. 'Poor Gaby! She set such store by that marriage to Evan, and he died and left her so soon. You know, if it hadn't been for her, I don't suppose I'd ever have met Charles again.'

'Again?' Patricia looked eagerly at Mary, sensing a story. It would be more interesting than her dreary past.

'Yes. I knew Charles and Maggie slightly when I was a gauche schoolgirl. We belonged to the same tennis club. Then I went nursing, met and married Tony, my first husband—Mrs Hughes's son—and had Toinette.

'Tony was always a bit of a rolling stone. I'd thought he took after Gaby's family, but I've discovered that all

74

the Verity men are a bit wild in one way or another. I'd always been worried that Toinette would take after her father, but it seems that the Verity women have the share of stability that was left out when the Verity men had their virtues doled out.'

'How did you meet Charles again, then?' asked Patricia.

'Oh, that came some time after Gaby remarried. When Tony was killed in the Congo—did you know, he went up there as a mercenary?—I went back to work—full-time nursing. I had finished my basic training and my Midwifery before I married Tony. Gaby came to live with us and to look after Toinette. You can't do full-time nursing unless you've someone reliable to leave your child with. The hours aren't really any longer than other people's, but they're irregular. You have to work late two or three nights a week unless you've a clinic job or are doing District work. Or you have to go on night duty. It would be impossible to do that and look after a little girl properly unless there was someone to take over when you're on duty.

'When Gaby married Evan, I decided to do private duty nursing. That way, I could work all the term and be able to spend all the school holidays with Toinette.'

'What happened during term-time, then?' asked Patricia.

'Oh, that was when I sent her to boarding school. I worked for our livings while she was at school, and at the beginning of the holidays I'd fetch her from D.S.G. and we'd enjoy ourselves, until the beginning of the next term. One term, I was sent here to Blouvlei to look after Charles and his father. Charles had had an accident—his truck had skidded off a wet road when there was a washaway that no one had warned him about. He had spinal injuries and was at the Lady Michaelis Hospital, Capetown, for ages, and although

75

his father hadn't been with him—the old man was doing less and less, in fact that was intended to be his last expedition—the old man was considerably shocked by it all.

'When Charles was discharged and came home a cripple, it was too much for Maggie, and Paul van der Berg, their family doctor, told her to apply for a private duty Sister to come and help cope. I was the Sister.'

'And the two of you fell in love.' Patricia spoke dreamily. It was in the best traditions of the happy endings in the novels of her favourite Josephine Cantrell.

'Not immediately.' Mary laughed. 'There were quite a lot of misunderstandings and so on first. Toinette would have liked it that way. She always thought it romantic that I should meet a man on whom I'd had a schoolgirl crush at the age of sixteen or seventeen. Then she developed appendicitis in the middle of term, and had to have it out, and as her convalescence occurred right in the middle of term, when it would mean that the Milsteads would have to get another relief, they invited her here. Toinette loved every moment and got horribly spoiled. She had her fourteenth birthday here, and marked Charles down as a stepfather at once. I must say hers and Charles's is one of the happiest "step" relationships I've ever come across, thank goodness.'

Patricia envied all three of them, and the baby. She had seldom encountered a more happy family, even in her Aunt Gwennie's home.

As if reading her thoughts, Mary asked, 'Do you often hear from your aunt?'

'Sometimes. Although I was quite a help with the children, I think she's really relieved that I've found a job out here. It's one thing to have a niece on tap who can come round and babysit at weekends and in the Easter holidays, and quite another to have that niece descend upon you without two beans to rub together, and no job in the offing either. Aunt Gwennie's husband's always been hard up, and as far as one can see, always will be.'

Patricia had also heard from Richard Horton— friendly, interested letters. His first had been in answer to her bread-and-butter letter, telling him that she had arrived safely and that everything was going smoothly so far.

Write again, he had written. *I know I've landed you with a job that doesn't leave much time for writing. My sister always used to ask me how I expected her to write more when she had three young imps to look after. But drop me a line when you've time, and let me know how things are going. And don't think I'm asking this in a sort of policeman frame of mind, because I'm not. Naturally, I want to know how my niece and nephews are getting on, but I also want to know how you're getting on. After all, I did rather pitchfork you into the job without finding out what you felt about it. I'd hate to think you were miserable, and felt yourself cut off from everything, stuck out there in the bundu.*

After due reflection, Patricia had replied that the children were very well indeed, and seemed perfectly happy. Everything was running smoothly, and the two elder children seemed to be doing well enough at school, from what their teachers said. She added that she was quite well, thank you, and after a little more reflection, added that she was extremely happy and was loving the life, and that she was far from being cut off. She had never dreamed that there was such a lot going on in a little dorp like Blouvlei.

It was perfectly true; there was far more social life than there was in a big city. Here, everyone knew everyone else, and as she was looking after the children of a couple who had been popular in the district, she found herself being invited out more and more. When the children were included, she had no scruples in accepting. After all, she felt that they were the reason for the invitation, and that they ought to be given the opportunity to meet their parents' friends.

When she was asked out alone, however, she invariably refused, politely, gratefully, but firmly. She had been employed to care for the three children, and care for them she would. She had made up her mind to justify Richard Horton's faith in her, and she would do that if it killed her.

It was Mary Milstead who changed her mind for her.

' Of course you must go and play tennis,' she said. ' Leave the children with me for the afternoon. Richard didn't mean you to be chained to them night and day. You must have a break.'

It was the same when she was invited to attend the weekly film show in an old hall, and when she was invited to join a party of young people at a dance. She mentioned it rather apologetically in one of her informative letters to her employer. His reply showed that he agreed with Mary Milstead.

Of course you must get out and have a change. Looking after kids is a trying job, however much you enjoy it and like them. Even their own mother needed a break now and then. As long as you make sure that there is someone responsible in charge, that's the main thing, and I know Mary Milstead or Maggie van der Berg would help you to find someone even if they weren't able to oblige themselves. Good heavens, girl, it's your job, and no one's expected to be on continuous duty twenty-four hours a day without a break sometimes. Enjoy yourself. I'm glad you're happy, and I'm glad you're making friends in Blouvlei.

This letter touched Patricia so much that Mary Milstead, coming over to ask her to bring Podge over for morning tea, found her in tears.

'My dear, what's the matter?' asked Mary. 'Not bad news?'

'Wonderful!' Patricia sat up and scrubbed her eyes. 'I'm stupid, I know, but it's so lovely to have someone glad one's happy, it just got me. And when you think of the way I was going on when he found me! Read this!' She thrust the letter towards Mary.

'He's a good sort,' said Mary when she had read the letter. 'It sometimes takes people a little time to find that out, because of his dry manner. Lots of people don't think he has a sense of humour, either. And I wouldn't worry about what you were doing when he found you. Obviously he doesn't.'

'But you simply don't know,' wailed Patricia.

Mary did not say that she did know. It would be tactless in the extreme to let the girl know that she and Richard had discussed her in letters. Evidently Patricia was determined to get it all off her chest. Peter was safely in his playpen under the watchful eye of Charles, who was sketching him as a change from a family of sunbirds. Mary sat down and prepared to listen.

When Patricia had finished her recital, Mary smiled. 'It wasn't so very terrible really,' she said. 'After all, it was more Simon's fault than yours. He took advantage of the fact that you didn't know where to turn for money and hadn't anything to live on, and also that at that time you were still suffering from shock after the accident to your mother and stepfather and all that came afterwards. Dick's a pretty good judge of character, and as he said, often plays his hunches. You'd be surprised how often they work out—like the one that concerned you. Now go and wash your face and put on a bit of make-up and you and Podge are coming over to have a cup of tea with us. Where is Podge?'

'On the back stoep. In his playpen.'

'Has Dick said anything about when he's coming?' asked Charles over a cup of tea, having given up trying to make sketches of two lively toddlers.

'No, not to me. Is he coming?' asked Patricia, to whom the question had been addressed.

'He usually spends Christmas here in Blouvlei,' said Charles. 'He always used to stay with Martha and Jim.'

'Well, he can't very well stay next door now,' commented Mary, 'not without a chaperon. You know what gossip's like in a place like Blouvlei. If you sneeze at one end, there's a thunderstorm at the other.'

For some reason, Patricia felt herself blushing. She hoped that the Milsteads would not notice. Apparently they did not.

'I must ask Maggie if she's heard from him,' said Mary. 'After all, she's got more spare room in her house than either Pat or we have. Besides, Ann's coming for Christmas, so our only spare room will be filled. Ann's my aunt,' she said, turning to Patricia. 'She's a Charge Sister at the Jan Smuts Hospital, Southcliff, where I trained.'

'You'd never think she was a Ward Sister when you meet her off duty.' Charles grinned reminiscently. 'Do you remember when she came up for our wedding? She had Dad on his feet and waltzing with her, and he wasn't a bit the worse for it. Said he wished he'd met her ten years before.'

'She's got a wicked sense of humour,' said Mary. 'She always used to enjoy the situation on the quiet when I had to work in her ward and call her " Sister " most respectfully, when all the time we were both remembering something that we'd laughed at or an argument we'd had the evening before.'

'It's a good thing *she's* not staying with the van der Bergs,' commented Charles. 'She'd have her nose in a book all over Christmas if she was. She says that there are at least half a dozen of Maggie's books that she hasn't caught up with yet. It's extraordinary how Maggie's books go down with the most intelligent people.'

' How do you mean, Maggie's books?' asked Patricia. ' She's got quite a varied selection.'

' But more of Josephine Cantrell's than anyone else's,' said Charles.

' Yes, she has a good many of them,' said Patricia, ' not that I mind. I love Josephine Cantrell's books, and I've had a lovely time borrowing them. She's one of my favourite writers.'

' Maggie will be pleased,' said Charles, his smile a little mocking, his voice very kind. ' It's her pseudonym. She *is* Josephine Cantrell.'

' She's *what*?' Patricia was almost struck dumb. ' You can't mean that? Not really?'

' It's true. She's dreadfully modest about it, though. It's her bad luck that she's the daughter of a man who made a name for himself writing natural history textbooks. If Dad hadn't been who he was, Maggie'd never have had the inferiority complex that she has about her books. And Dad was always immensely proud of her successes.'

This piece of information went into Patricia's next letter to Dick, after she had told him all that he ought to know about the children's progress:

Peggy came first in Arithmetic last week. Her teacher is really pleased with her. David fell and cut his knee and had to have stitches in it. He did it at school trying to climb on to the roof of the grandstand on the sports field. I had an awful fright when they rang up to ask me to fetch him home. I was relieved, though, that he did it at school. If it had happened at home, I'd have found it hard to forgive myself. As it is—well, the school authorities are more used to that kind of

*responsibility than I am. They didn't seem to think
anything of it. The master I saw just said, ' Boys will
be boys.' They put in three stitches and gave him anti-
tetanus serum. That gave him nettlerash, but not badly.
It went down when Paul van der Berg gave him another
injection. I think David rather enjoyed all the fuss!*

*By the way, did you know that Maggie van der Berg
is Josephine Cantrell, the author? I nearly had a fit!
She's so modest and unassuming. Charles and Mary say
it's because their father was the G. O. C. Milstead, who
wrote all those gorgeous natural history books. She's
given me an autographed copy of her latest*—A Quiet
Holiday. *Isn't that sweet of her?*

*I really am sorry about David's knee, but he's really
all right. . . .*

She had no idea how much of herself she was showing
to Richard Horton by her letters about the children. She
was revealing herself, not as the spoiled, sophisticated
little brat that she had appeared in the sleazy hotel in
Capetown, but as a natural, loving girl, who for the first
time in her life had found stability and good friends and
a home. He wrote back a long, kind letter, telling her
not to worry any more about David's knee. From what
he remembered of his own boyhood, no one could stop
small boys from knocking themselves about, and there
would be something wrong with them if one could.

He was glad that she liked Maggie Milstead's books.
They were excellent of their kind. He had known the
Milsteads for a good many years, he wrote, and as well
as being a talented family, they were all pleasant,
unassuming people.

He would, he said, be seeing her soon, as he had been
invited to spend Christmas with the Van der Bergs.

Patricia was singing as she pushed Podge in his push-
chair into the dorp to do her morning shopping. Podge
joined in with a happy, tuneless humming.

CHAPTER VI

Gradually, as Patricia settled down to her routine at Number Five, Green Street, she found herself relaxing. She had not realised how tense she had been, that the shock of her mother's death with her stepfather, and the revelation of his guilt that followed it had gone on. Now, at last, she was beginning to feel really happy, and as though she belonged somewhere.

She was desperately keen to make a success of looking after the young Collins children. If Richard Horton approved of the way in which she was bringing them up, perhaps she could stay on until young Podge was old enough not to need a woman to care for him. That would not be for a good many years yet, and she was glad. She did not want this life to come to an end, although she realised that it must, some time.

Her life hitherto had made a realist out of her. Obviously, this life would not go on for ever. The only woman who can be in close contact with a group of children whom she has cared for once they are grown up is their mother. A paid employee would be expected to find another job once the last of the children could fend for himself.

Well, she was completely untrained, and had not the educational qualifications to train for most of the well-paid professions, so although it would be madness to dwell on the lonely future that would be hers when the children grew up and away from her, she must be practical. The salary that Richard was paying her was more than generous. She could save plenty for a rainy day.

She was amazed at herself for liking the place so much. She had never seen much of the Eastern Cape, but had not liked what she had seen very much. The great mountains of the Western Province had been more to her liking, and the old buildings in the city of Cape-town itself, and the old homesteads nestling in the mountains. The Eastern Cape had seemed so bare and open as they drove along the roads in Garth's Panhard. The Garden Route, from the Cape to Port Elizabeth, running through the Knysna Forest, was beautiful, but when you left that, and drove over bare golden veld, with hardly a tree except when you passed through dorps of white and cream-washed cottages with corrugated iron or asbestos roofs, shaded by gum trees, it all seemed so new.

From some unknown ancestor, Patricia had inherited a sense of the past. Capetown was not as old as the villages that she had known in England. Even the busy cities held beauties hundreds of years old. She remembered Gloucester Cathedral with its Norman arches, and the little old places hidden away, upon which one came unexpectedly when one was wandering through the bustling little city.

Capetown went back for more than three hundred years, and to her mind, had a continuity with the past that was not found in the Eastern Cape, which had not been colonised until a little over a hundred and fifty years ago. She had loved Capetown.

Now, right away from the Mother City, she realised that her feelings had changed while she had had so much on her mind that she had not thought about her surroundings very much. She realised, in this little dorp, little more than one street, with its plain little houses, none of them of any historical interest, that the sky-scrapers which had been springing up in Capetown like mushrooms during the past years, had seemed to shut out the sky. Here, it was a great arc overhead, sometimes hard and blue, sometimes with rolling clouds chasing across it, but untrammelled and free, the only things

84

that shut it out or altered the horizon being a *koppie*, the shoulder of a mountain or a group of trees.

Here, on stable ground once more, she realised that the tremors that had shaken Capetown intermittently ever since the earthquakes that had destroyed many homes in Tulbagh, in the mountains behind the city, a year or two back, had worked on her nerves more than she had realised at the time.

The dashing back and forth from England to Capetown and back as a child had made for a lack of stability —the kind of stability that, giving it to the Collins children, she was now experiencing herself. The brittle, gay, sophisticated young people who had formed her circle— young people like Simon Verity—who had been introduced to her by her mother, and whom, before the crash, she had thought of as her friends, all seemed trivial in the extreme when compared with the people she had met since she arrived at Blouvlei. They in their turn, she realised, would have found people like Mary Milstead, Maggie van der Berg and their husbands, and even young Antoinette Verity, too dull for words.

To Patricia's surprise, she had even started going more or less regularly to church in Blouvlei. She had been confirmed while still at school, and had gone every Sunday during term-time with her grandmother, but never when at home with her mother and stepfather. The idea had never entered her head or theirs.

But the Collins children went every Sunday. Mary and Patricia took it in turns to take the young ones to Sunday School at ten o'clock, and the one who was staying at home then went to Communion at eight. Mary had taken it so much for granted that Patricia would go that she had done just that, feeling at first a little self-conscious, and wondering what had got into her. Then, although she never liked the initial plunge out of bed, she came to enjoy the service, and to make friends with the others who went.

Sometimes she met Maggie van der Berg there. Brought up an Anglican herself, Maggie had married a husband who belonged to the Dutch Reformed Church, the church of the Afrikaner. Nearly every Sunday she went with him to the later service of his church, but most weeks she had already been to Early Service in her own church. At Christmas and Easter, she told Patricia, he would come with her.

Christmas was nearly here. Ann Burns, Mary Milstead's aunt, who was a Sister at the hospital in Southcliff, had thirty days' leave, and had arrived in the evening of December the first. Antoinette would be home from school in Grahamstown on the fifteenth, for the last time. Peggy and David would be at home all day, except when they were out on one of the expeditions arranged for the young people during the long summer holidays.

Richard Horton was spending Christmas with the Van der Bergs.

Patricia was not so sure how she felt about meeting him again. She had thoroughly enjoyed his letters, feeling deprived if one did not arrive on the day it ought to arrive. But letters were one thing; the man's physical presence was another. Was he really as good-looking as she remembered? Would he still look as stern and as disapproving as he had done when she had met him in Capetown? Would he think that the children were looking well and decently dressed? Especially, she thought, the latter. They looked well enough, although Peggy had sustained a black eye, falling out of the loquat tree in the garden.

With memories of first-aid lectures in mind, Patricia had been unable to rid herself of the fear that the black eye just *might* be caused by extravasation of blood into the tissues from a fractured skull. Mary had tried to reassure her, but after the applications of butter and raw steak, had agreed that it might do no harm for her to see Paul van der Berg.

'It's only a simple black eye,' he had said, 'but if it'll set your mind at rest, we'll get it X-rayed.' So he had run the two of them up to the Cottage Hospital, and worked the little X-ray camera himself, after which he was able to prove to Patricia that Peggy had no fracture of the skull.

The black eye was fading nicely. Patricia hoped that it would have disappeared altogether by the time that Richard arrived, two days before Christmas Eve.

It was the day before Richard's arrival that nearly drove Patricia out of her mind. Podge was fretful with teething; he usually became miserable when a tooth was coming through, and knowing that it would only last for a day or two, Patricia was able to bear with him. Angelina was being chivvied into unwanted activity, polishing and cleaning everything that could be made to shine, and to scrub and dust everything else in the house. At last it was even beginning to satisfy Patricia, who felt that all it needed now was a last-minute sweeping and dusting just before Richard arrived.

True, he was not staying at Green Street; for him to stay at Number Five with no more adequate chaperon than the children would be unwise. The household at Number Three would be full in any case, with Antoinette home, and Ann Burns a house-guest. The childless Van der Bergs with their double-storey house were the obvious hosts. But Patricia was sure that as soon as he had settled in, and as soon as it was reasonably polite to leave his host and hostess, he would come up to inspect the home of his niece and nephews, and see how the girl whom he had put in charge was doing her job.

Richard was due to arrive in Blouvlei on December

the twenty-first. On the twentieth, Angelina did not come to work, neither did she, as was traditional, send someone else in her place. Mary offered to send Rosie over to give a hand, but Patricia refused.

'I'll manage, thanks,' she said. 'I've got everything so well in hand that there's only a flip round with a duster to be done, and to put a few flowers in the vases. No, you keep Rosie; you've a house full, and Peggy and David spend more time with their friends than they do at home now the holidays have started. I'll manage Podge all right; he's happy for hours in his playpen with a few toys.'

But that was just what Podge would not do. On the morning of the twenty-first, Patricia, with Podge clinging to one hip, had waved to Peggy and David, who were going for an all-day picnic with friends before turning to put the toddler into his playpen before getting on with the washing up. But Podge would not stay in his playpen. Instead of sitting down and playing with his favourite disreputable old stuffed rabbit and his wooden engine, he stood clinging to the bars and howling dismally until Patricia picked him up.

Obviously she could get on with no work while she was carrying him about, but she discovered to her relief that he would keep quiet as long as he could follow her about. It was a great nuisance, as she had to have eyes in the back of her head to see that he came to no harm.

The breakfast things washed up, she gathered the children's dirty clothes and put them in the washing machine. A young girl, a daughter of Angelina, came every Monday to do the week's wash—the sheets, towels, tablecloths and the heavy wash. She did it all quite early in the morning, starting while her mother was still cooking the breakfast. She came back in the afternoon to do the ironing, for unless it rained, the washing dried quickly in the dry up-country air. But there were always extras—Podge's napkins and rompers, David's shorts and socks, Peggy's school blouses and frocks. Patricia had very soon discovered that unless she had a minor wash every day, or every other day, the children would not have enough to wear, and neither, for that matter, would she.

At first, apart from trying to climb into the washing machine, Podge behaved in an exemplary manner. Patricia hauled him off, closed and set the machine and turned it on before taking him, his toy engine and the vacuum cleaner into the lounge. Here, at first, everything went with a swing. Patricia was making good time. It was only a little after ten o'clock. She did not know what time Richard was expected, but he would hardly come up here straight away; even if he arrived before lunch, presumably, he would have morning tea and his midday meal with the Van der Bergs. He'd probably arrive at Green Street in time for afternoon tea, she thought.

She finished the floor, took out the vacuum cleaner, took the clothes out of the washing machine and, closely followed by Podge, hung them on the line before fetching a duster and going back to dust the lounge.

'I'll do the dining-room while the lunch is cooking,' she said to an unresponsive Podge.

The previous evening, she had arranged some roses from the garden in an attractive brass trough that she had found, and had put them on the carved wooden mantelpiece in the lounge. This morning, going to dust the ornaments on the mantelpiece, she found that it was sopping wet, and that the water had stained the wood.

'Oh—!' She glanced round at the silent Podge and thought better of what she had been going to say. Podge was not talking fluently yet, but he was very imitative. It would never do if he came out with a swear-word that she had learned from her Capetown 'friends' in front

89

of his Uncle Richard!.

She would have to find something else for the roses when she had the time. Meanwhile, the mantelpiece would have to be polished. She ran out to the kitchen with the leaking rose-trough, and came back with the polish.

All was quiet while she took the ornaments off. Putting polish on the stained wood, she forgot to watch him, he was so quiet. It was when she was starting to try and bring up the shine with a clean duster that Podge startled her by giving an anguished wail. Dropping her duster and wheeling round, she saw that he had somehow wedged himself under the sofa and was stuck.

It was a ponderous, old-fashioned piece of furniture, and its base was very near the ground. She could not imagine how Podge had managed to insert himself into such a small space in the first place, nor how she was going to get him out. On hands and knees, she pondered, talking soothingly to the howling Podge as she did so.

' It's all right, Podgey, Padda'll get you out, though goodness knows how I'll do it. If I pull you out, I'll hurt you. All right, sweetie, we'll soon have you out. But I'll need both hands to lift the darn thing, and when I do, how'll I know that you'll crawl in the right direction? You'll probably just sit there, and as the damn sofa's heavy, I'll probably drop it on you and kill you. No, the only thing is for me to try and lift it far enough to crawl underneath a little way myself, and hold it up on my shoulders for long enough to shove you out.'

Somehow she managed to lift the weight of the heavy sofa and crawl underneath it. In her concern for Podge, she was hardly aware that the weight was lifted from her shoulders so that instead of pushing him out of the way before crawling out herself, she was able to back out with Podge in her arms.

She knelt there hugging, kissing and scolding him. 'Oh, Podge darling, how could you do a thing like that to me? It's all right, pet; you haven't hurt yourself, only given yourself a fright. Well, that settles it; you'll just have to stay in the playpen now, even if you do howl the place down. I can't cope with anything like that again, not if I'm to get my work done!'

Still clutching Podge to her, Patricia rolled round and up on to her feet, to find Richard Horton laughing down at her. Momentarily, she was bereft of speech. Not so Podge. With outstretched arms, he chortled, 'Dig! Dig!' Like his brother and sister, he seldom used the titles 'aunt' and 'uncle,' and this was the nearest that he could get to his uncle's name.

'Hello, old chap, been getting into mischief?' Richard relieved Patricia of her burden.

'He's probably wet,' warned Patricia.

'I'm not wearing anything that'll spoil,' said Richard. He was wearing a pair of immaculate grey flannels, and a snowy-white open-necked silk shirt. He looked far smarter, thought Patricia, than most of the men she met, who almost without exception wore either a khaki bush-shirt and shorts, or, as a slight variation, a brightly checked shirt. Nearly all of them wore bright blue socks. She thought he looked quite devastatingly and disturbingly handsome. She had forgotten, if she had noticed at the time, what a good-looking man he was.

'Have—have you been there for long?' she asked.

'Not very long. I came in in time to see you wriggling like a snake under the sofa. Honestly, I don't know how you did it. I wouldn't have thought there was enough space for a tiddler like Podge, let alone a grown woman!'

'That was just the trouble,' said Patricia bitterly. 'There wasn't room for Podge. He got stuck. And the place is in a dreadful mess!' She was ready to burst into tears. 'And I meant to have it looking spick and span by the time you arrived!'

'Don't worry.' His face and voice were so kind that it was almost the finish of Patricia. 'I think you look as if you could do with a cup of tea, and I'm sure I could. I left Southcliff at seven, and I've not stopped on the way. Mary's Aunt Ann would say I'm thoroughly dehydrated. Suppose you make us a cup while I keep this young devil amused.'

'Debbil, debbil. Podge Debbil. Padda debbil!' Podge was enchanted with this lovely new word.

'He copies everything one says,' said Patricia. 'I find I have to be dreadfully careful.' She was relieved to see that instead of being shocked, Richard appeared to be amused.

'I—I'll go and get the tea,' she said, annoyed to find that she seemed to have developed a stammer in Richard's presence since the last time she had met him.

When she came back with the tea-tray, she found Podge almost asleep in his uncle's arms.

'I'll put him in his cot,' she said, putting down the tray. 'He didn't get much sleep last night. He's teething, and it's making him *impossible*, poor little sausage. An extra nap won't do him any harm.'

'I'll carry him,' said Richard, getting up carefully. 'Where's his cot?'

'In here.' Patricia preceded him into her own room, thankful that she had made her bed and at least done the minimum of tidying when she got up that morning, knowing that it would be some time before she could get back to it. She had never in her wildest dreams thought that Richard would come in here!

They said no more after depositing the now deeply slumbering Podge into his cot until Patricia had poured out tea for them both. Richard drank his at one gulp and handed her the cup for more.

' That was certainly good,' he said. ' Where are the other two?'

' Gone for a picnic up the mountain with the Van der Meschts.'

' And you stayed at home like Cinderella.' It was a statement, not a question.

' Not quite.' Patricia was beginning to recover herself, and gave him a wicked grin. ' Cinderella didn't have a teething toddler to contend with. If she had, she mightn't have been so eager to dance. She'd have been too tired.'

' Podge too much for you?' he asked, lighting his pipe.

' Too much? Good lord, no! He's a darling. Never a dull moment.' Patricia leapt to Podge's defence. She thought it was time to start giving him the news of the other two.

' David's well, and came top in his form at the end of term. Peggy was third. She—she fell out of the loquat tree just before the end of term. She—she wasn't badly hurt. She got a black eye, but it's almost faded. I took her to Dr van der Berg, and he said he didn't think it was much. He X-rayed her at the Cottage Hospital and there was no fracture.' The words came tumbling out.

Richard laughed. ' I cut my head open when I fell out of that tree,' he said. ' It's not much now; you can hardly see it, but it bled like a stuck pig, and I had six stitches in it.' He pointed to a scar on his forehead as fine as a hair.

' And why,' he asked, ' are you killing yourself with housework? Where's your girl? Haven't you got one?'

' We have, but she just didn't turn up yesterday or today. Normally, I'd have let things slide a bit, but I wanted the place to be looking decent when you arrived. Everything went wrong this morning! Podge is teething, as I told you, and wouldn't stay in his playpen. The flower vase leaked all over the mantelpiece, and then, while I was trying to get the wet marks off, Podge got himself stuck under the sofa. That's where you came in.'

Richard looked at his watch. 'Eleven o'clock. I looked in here first because I'm earlier than I'd said I'd be. Maggie van der Berg's not expecting me until one o'clock. Look, what are you going to do about your lunch? If you intended spending the morning cleaning, when were you going to cook?'

'If I hadn't been so long in here, I was going to put a joint in to do while I turned out the dining-room. Before you arrived, I'd already decided to do myself a chop and some frozen vegetables. I usually keep a few packets in the deep-freeze. It's convenient when we've been out and come in lateish. They're so quick.'

'Well, you're doing no such thing. I'm ringing Maggie up now and telling her that I'm on my way, and that I'm bringing you and Podge.'

'You can't wish the two of us on her at the last minute like this,' protested Patricia.

'You don't know Maggie,' said Richard. 'She'll be delighted.'

'But what about Podge's lunch? He has Purity foods.'

'What—oh, those funny little messes in jars? They don't take much preparation, do they?'

'N—no, not really. They just need heating up, but . . .'

'Well, go and wash your face and hands and collect a pot of Podge's lunch while I give Maggie a tinkle. Go on!'

'Suppose Podge doesn't behave himself? He's been dreadfully grizzly the last day or two with that tooth.'

'We'll get Paul to give him a sedative if he gets too stroppy. I never met such a girl for making difficulties!'

Patricia went.

As she collected a jar of meat and vegetable purée and one of apple purée, and remembered to put half a dozen napkins into a plastic bag, washed her hands and face and slapped on some make-up, she overheard snatches of Richard's conversation with Maggie Milstead.

'Yes, left earlier than I intended and got here at a little after ten . . . yes, thought I'd look in here first, on my way . . . yes, well, Maggie, can you have Pat and Podge for lunch? . . . You can? . . . No, nothing wrong. The kids have gone for a picnic, she says . . . Yes, being a handful, I gather . . . I got there to find her trying to rescue him from under the sofa . . . Wouldn't stay there . . . Too conscientious? . . . Yes, that was the impression I got . . . All right, thanks, Mag. Expect us in about ten minutes. . . . 'Bye now.'

Patricia was standing in the doorway of her bedroom, her handbag and the plastic bag with Podge's effects in her hands, fresh and pretty in a clean green linen frock, bare brown legs and white sandals. Her hair, which as she had washed it the previous evening, was unruly, she had tied back with a matching green ribbon. The still-sleeping Podge was in his carrycot at her feet.

Patricia was surprised to realise how much she enjoyed her lunch at the Van der Bergs'. For one thing, it was a change of scene. Every day since she had come to Blouvlei, she had eaten her midday meal with the three Collins children at Number Five, except when they had gone for a picnic by the Municipal dam. She often went next door to tea in the afternoon, but even if Peggy went to friends, Podge always and David nearly always came too. True, she sometimes went out dancing or to a film on a Saturday night, but it was not always easy to find a babysitter, and she did not like to ask Mary Milstead too often. It meant that she had to leave Charles alone in Number Three watching their own baby, and

95

nor did she like to impose on Maggie van der Berg's kindness too often.

The lunch was hilarious. Maggie had a delicious sense of humour, and her husband every now and then would make a pawky joke. Richard's humour was dry but kindly. Patricia had thought that she would spend the meal in tongue-tied awe of him, but he drew her out to talk.

To her relief, Podge, tired after a restless night and an eventful morning, did not wake until they had finished their own meal, and then, just as Maggie's maid brought in the coffee, he stirred.

'Minah,' said Maggie, 'have you warmed the baby's food like I told you?'

'*Eywe*, missis.'

'And it's not too hot?'

'*Ai*, missis.'

'All right, bring it in, then, and warm some milk and have it ready. I suppose Podge does drink out of a mug, Pat?'

'Oh yes; he's fine. He only has a bottle at night when he's going to sleep.'

Minah disappeared and came back with Podge's dinner on a tray in little plastic dishes. Patricia picked him up, and, finding that he was wet, took a napkin out of her bag.

'I'd better change him in the bathroom,' she said.

When she had gone out, Maggie turned to Richard.

'Satisfied with what you've found?' she asked.

'The only thing wrong is that Pat's looking worn out,' he said. 'I'm wondering if I did the right thing, not for the kids, but for her. I haven't seen the other two yet, but teething or not, Podge looks the picture of health.'

'I don't think you need worry about her,' said Maggie. 'She'll be able to relax a bit when the holidays are over, but I'll have to find her a maid until Angelina pitches up again. Don't worry. Minah'll know of someone. We do think that Pat's a bit over-conscientious, as I've said, and that she doesn't get enough fun, but she always seems happy enough, and she doesn't always look as tired as she does today. After all, Podge isn't teething all the time. If she hadn't got this job—if you hadn't had the hunch that she might do for the children, what would she have done?'

'God knows! Her mother seems to have let her grow up utterly unequipped to deal with life. She'd have been all right if her stepfather hadn't turned out a crook and then gone and killed himself and her mother with dangerous driving. I don't know what she'd have done, Maggie.'

'Then don't worry about her, Richard. You did the children a good turn when you found her; they love her and she looks after them as though they were her own. And you did her a good turn too. You gave her a job she loves, with a home thrown in, and it'll go on for years unless something very unforeseen happens. It'll go on until the children grow up, unless she meets someone she wants to marry.'

Richard looked startled. 'I hadn't thought of that,' he said.

They could not say any more as Patricia bore Podge back into the room clean and wholesome and ready for his lunch.

Paul van der Berg left them to do his afternoon visits. Maggie and Richard withdrew to the window while Patricia sat at the table, Podge on her knee, utterly absorbed, not hearing what the other two adults were talking about.

'She'll make some man a wonderful wife one day,' said Maggie softly, 'and she'll be a wonderful mother. And I don't think it'll be so far off either.'

Q V—D 97

' But she's just a kid herself,' protested Richard.

' She's nearly twenty-two, Dick.'

' Has she anyone in view?'

' Not that I know of, surprisingly enough. When she *does* manage to get out and have fun, she's very much in demand, so I hear, but the children are her whole life at the moment. I think it's because it's the first bit of real home life she's had for years, poor child. But one of these days, she'll want a home of her own. For the children's sake, I hope it won't be until they don't need her any longer, because you won't find anyone else who devotes herself to them as Pat does. For her sake, I hope she doesn't leave it too long.'

Richard looked across the room at Patricia coaxing Podge to eat, absorbed and happy, utterly oblivious of anything else. He saw her with new eyes. For the first time, he saw her as a woman, and a desirable woman at that.

CHAPTER VII

To Patricia, Christmas seemed like a dream. Never before had she experienced a real traditional Christmas, at least not since she had been old enough to remember. Always, she had been flown out from the bitter English winter to her mother in the Cape, at first in the charge of a stewardess, and later under her own steam, with injunctions not to speak to strange men. Once there, there had been parties and gaiety, but not like this; more sophisticated gaiety, with more grown-ups than childen, and often some of the grown-ups having had more than they could comfortably carry of the drinks on the table.

She would rather, even then, have been left alone to play with the toys that she had been given, under the watchful eye of Tienie, her nurse-girl, but instead, she had been dragged to functions and parties that were much too old for her. Garth, always afraid that his wife would feel that he wanted to push her daughter out of things, insisted that she was brought along too, and her mother had acquiesced.

This year, for the first time, she was part and parcel of a proper Christmas, the king-pin and pivot on which depended the enjoyment of three children. She was determined that they would have a Christmas to remember.

On Mary Milstead's advice, they cooked the turkey the day before, and made salads, delectable salads which Patricia had learned to make during her year's study of domestic science, but here in South Africa there were so many more ingredients—paw-paw, fresh pineapple instead of the tinned variety, avocado pears.

On Christmas morning Richard arrived early to take Patricia and Peggy down to the early service. Mary was to keep an eye on David and Podge, and would go down at eleven o'clock to the later service, when Patricia would keep an eye on her small son. At the last minute, Antoinette came over and slipped into the back of Richard's Wolseley.

'I didn't ask you to give me a lift in,' she said breathlessly, 'because I was afraid I might oversleep, but I didn't. Mom says I can help you keep an eye on the little ones during the morning, and it'll be easier for you to supervise getting dinner if there are two of us. Oh, by the way, Merry Christmas!'

Richard spent the morning with them as well, staying for breakfast and then asking Patricia if there was enough lunch for him.

'Of course,' said Patricia, 'we'll love to have you with us, but won't the Van der Bergs be expecting you?'

'No, they left it to me. I told Maggie I'd a fancy for eating Christmas dinner with my own folk. The kids are the nearest blood relations I've got, and I want them to regard me as their own. It's awkward that I can't have them with me—a bachelor household isn't an ideal place to bring up three youngsters, especially a little girl, and I think they're better off here in the home they're used to, with you. But I like to turn up now and then so that they don't forget about Uncle Dick.'

Patricia laughed. 'They're not likely to do that. You should just hear them talking when you're expected.'

'Tea up!' Antoinette called from the hall. 'Outside on the back stoep.'

Podge refused to stay in his playpen. He was getting more and more firm on his feet every day, and wanted to go everywhere. Patricia had to lift him out, or he would have had the playpen over on top of himself.

'I'll either have to have a gate made at the top of the steps,' she said, 'or get a bigger, heavier playpen made. I never saw such a child! But if it's a gate, I'll have to see that they put a really safe fastening on it. The other day he got out and went down the path to the front gate. I only just reached him before he managed to open it. He'll have me grey before my time!' She regarded the toddler affectionately. 'We shan't be able to call him Podge much longer if he gets any more energetic; he'll work pounds off himself at this rate.'

'You love him very much, don't you, Pat?' said Richard.

'I just adore him,' answered Patricia. 'Who wouldn't?'

'When I marry,' said Antoinette, 'I shall have a dozen.'

Richard laughed. 'Won't your husband have something to say about that?'

'I shall find out first,' she said. 'All those answers to correspondents in the women's magazines tell people that they ought to find out that kind of thing before they get married. I shall only marry a man who's fond of children.'

With an odd little sinking feeling at her heart, which she could not explain to herself, Patricia wondered if Richard would consider Antoinette Verity too young for him, or conversely, if she would think him too old for her. She was just seventeen, and a very pretty seventeen, and Richard was nearly thirty-one. Patricia wondered why he had never married. In South Africa, men tended to marry earlier than they did in England, she had noticed, and a bachelor of Richard's age was fairly rare.

When the church contingent arrived home at a little after midday, Antoinette slipped through a gap in the garden fence to join her own family. Patricia egged on Minah, Angelina's successor, and they had their cold lunch early. There was a fine Nederberg Riesling, provided for the grown-ups by Richard, of which Peggy was allowed a sip, and there were ginger beer (home-made by Patricia) and various highly coloured cool drinks for David and Podge.

As soon as the meal was over, Patricia put Podge down to rest, and insisted that the other two lay down for a while. They were all invited down to the Van der Bergs for tea, supper and a Christmas tree. The Milsteads were going too, and the Scotts, whom Patricia had not yet met, were coming in from their farm, with their own two-year-old.

'You ought to get on with Erica Scott,' said Richard. 'She's from England—came out when she was a teen-ager, when her parents were killed on some scientific expedition or other. Her only relative was an aunt—her mother's much older sister. Mrs Webb—Erica's mother—was a South African. I believe Erica went to school in Cheltenham too, so you might even find that you know her.'

The Scotts had not arrived when the Green Street contingent were ushered into the large downstairs room at the Van der Bergs' home, where the party was to be held. Maggie looked a little put out.

'Erica rang and asked if she could bring their guest,' she told Richard. 'A Mrs Jorgens. I couldn't very well say no, but I don't like the sound of her.'

Richard laughed. 'It's not like you to judge people before you meet them, Mags.'

'Yes, but I know a bit about Lorraine Jorgens,' she said. 'You know the Shaws of Witvlerke in the Bosch-fontein District?'

Boschfontein was the nearest place to Blouvlei, about two hours' run in the car, and a much larger town, though small enough to be classed as a dorp.

'I know of them,' said Richard.

'Well,' went on Maggie, 'Fiona Shaw is Nick's second wife. From what I've heard, although I never knew

Beryl, I gather his first marriage was a disaster. Lorraine Jorgens is Beryl's sister, a divorcée, and nearly wrecked Fiona and Nick's romance before it started. When Nick found out what she was about, he practically threw her out of the house. Nowadays, she's *persona* very much *non grata* at Witvlerke, and I think, finds it hard to find somewhere to stay at Christmas, when even in the hotels, most people are wanting to be with their families. She's a very, very distant cousin of Andrew Scott's, and has foisted herself on them. Of course, I couldn't say I wouldn't have her, and even if I did, from what I've heard of her, she'd have come anyway.' She shrugged her shoulders resignedly. ' Well, there you are. But there are enough of us to have a good time without her spoiling things.'

They were out on the large stoep overlooking the Van der Bergs' garden when the Scotts arrived. Richard was down in the garden giving the two older Collins children swings, and Patricia and Mary Milstead were trying to make the toddlers have a good drink of milk so that they could be put down for an extra rest in their carrycots in Maggie van der Berg's big bedroom, so that they would not be too overtired to enjoy the Christmas tree later on.

Patricia heard the new guests coming towards the french doors, escorted by Maggie. She looked round, ready to be introduced. She liked the look of the Scotts. Andrew was big and dark, with slightly greying hair. Erica was fair, not much older than Patricia herself, and had a lively, happy look about her. Her little son Andy, coppery-haired and mischievous, clung to one hand.

' If I can give him a drink of milk with the other toddlers, Maggie,' she was saying, ' he'll probably sleep. He wouldn't rest this morning, and he's been like a little eel in the car.'

'I'll say he has!' The third member of the party came forward, a very smart, slim woman, attractive in a hard, well-groomed way, but certainly not pretty or even beautiful.

Her hair was almost the same colour as Patricia's but with more red, and without the gold glints that made Patricia's catch the sun. It was impeccably set, high on her head and back from her face. With her greenish-gold eyes, it gave her, thought Patricia, the look of a rather lovely but very untrustworthy vixen. She was evidently about to enlarge upon the behaviour of little Andy in the car, but suddenly stopped, her eyes riveted on Richard, where he was holding Peggy on the swing down in the garden. She turned to Maggie.

'My dear,' she purred, 'who *is* that gorgeous hunk of beefcake? Erica my dear, you never told me we'd be likely to run into this kind of talent!'

'That?' Maggie spoke carelessly, but Patricia could see that both she and young Mrs Scott were annoyed. They probably thought as she did, that it was an exhibition of arrant bad manners.

'That's Richard Horton,' said Maggie. 'His niece and nephews are two of the children who are the main reason for this party. Here's one of them.' She indicated the now quiet Podge, who had his face buried in an enormous mug of milk that Patricia was steadying for him.

'This is Pat Lang,' went on Maggie, performing introductions that she felt ought to come first. Richard could wait until his game with the other two was over. 'Pat's looking after the children for Richard. Pat, this is Erica and Andrew Scott and Mrs Jorgens.'

'Don't put the mug down to try and be polite,' said Erica Scott quickly as she saw Patricia's hand move. 'He'll never finish his milk once you break his concentration. I've found that out by bitter experience.' She sat

104

down on a spare chair, took up one of the empty mugs and filled it from the jug on the tray. 'All right, Maggie?'

'Of course, but don't you want your tea first?'

'I'd rather get this imp fed and then I can have it in peace.' She grabbed her son and gave him the milk, and soon the verandah was full of the contented sound of toddlers swallowing milk happily but far from silently. Mrs Jorgens looked disgruntled at being neglected, as Andrew Scott had run down to the garden to join Richard and the children.

'Do sit down, Mrs Jorgens. Won't you have some tea?' Maggie might not have wanted Mrs Jorgens, but she was not to be found wanting in hospitality. Lorraine sat down and accepted a cup, chatting in a rather bored way to Maggie and Erica, and completely ignoring Patricia. She was quite unaware that her chair was far too near Podge for her own safety. Having finished his milk, that young man looked up, and instead of swallowing the last mouthful, blew it out in one glorious raspberry, right on to the front of Lorraine's pale maize-coloured synthetic fibre frock.

'You little beast!' Lorraine leapt to her feet. 'As if that brat Andy's fingermarks weren't enough! They'll come out in the wash, but you can't get milk stains out!'

Patricia seized Podge and sprang apologetically to her feet.

'I am sorry,' she said. 'I ought to have been pre-pared, but this is a fairly new habit of his. I'm usually his target, though, so I never thought . . . Come on, Podge. Really, if it wasn't Christmas Day, I'd be tempted to give you a spanking!'

She disappeared into the house with Podge highly pleased with himself. She heard Maggie saying placat-ingly, 'Come into the bathroom. I think if we sponge it straight away with a clean cloth and cold water, before it dries, then it won't leave a stain.'

While she was changing Podge's napkin, she overheard the conversation in the bathroom, although she tried not to listen.

'Who *is* that girl?' asked Mrs Jorgens. 'Is she Richard Horton's wife?'

'Unfortunately not,' said Maggie. 'She's Pat Lang. When Richard's sister and brother-in-law both died within a very short time of one another, he was made their guardian. Mary Milstead—you met her just now out on the stoep with her husband Charles—you must have heard of him—he does those lovely little illustrated bird books? Well, they're old friends, and had the three children for a while, but Richard had a conscience about it. Mary's got a toddler of her own, and Charles isn't too strong after an accident that he had some years ago—he's my brother, by the way. Well, Richard happened to run up against Pat when she was out of a job and badly needing one. He needed someone to keep house here and look after the children, so that they could be cared for in their own home.'

'Taking a bit of a risk, wasn't he? What training has she had?'

'Very little, for a well-paid job in a city, but she's done a bit of domestic science, and has had some experience with children, so it seemed ideal, and it's turned out that way. She's done wonders with the children. I think if I just give it one more gentle rub with another clean cloth it ought to come out.

'Yes, losing both parents suddenly as they did could have been really traumatic, especially for the two elder ones, but since Pat's taken them over, they've become healthy, happy, normally naughty children. There, I think that's all we can do at the moment. I think it's all out, but we'll be able to tell better when it's dry.'

'I still think Richard Horton, did you say?—was taking a bit of a chance engaging that girl to look after those kids. After all, did he know anything of her antecedents?'

'She had connections with his family firm,' said Maggie, shortly for her.

'Ooh! Wait a minute! Now I get it. He must be one of the Hortons of Horton and Verity? Money as well as looks, *and* a bachelor. Then she must be the daughter —stepdaughter rather, of the man who was in all the papers a few months back—embezzled thousands and then committed suicide taking his wife with him. I suppose the wife was this girl's mother?'

'Yes!' Maggie was positively abrupt.

'Then I certainly think it unwise of Richard Horton to leave his wards in her charge. The daughter of a man who did a thing like that! What he needs is a wife who can see to their education and entertain for him as a director of a firm should.'

'What Pat's *step*father did can have no effect on her,' said Maggie firmly. 'There's no question of here-dity; there was no blood relationship. And if you're thinking of environment and influence, Pat spent most of her childhood at school in England, being looked after by a very strict grandmother. Come along and have some tea. I'm sure that skirt's going to dry all right.'

Pat waited until they were out of earshot. It would never do for her to appear too soon after they did; they could not then fail to realise that she had over-heard what they had been saying in the bathroom. Had she but known it, her thoughts were identical with those of Maggie at that moment. Both hoped that Richard Horton would have sufficient sense of self-preservation to keep out of the clutches of this predatory woman.

Patricia waited until she thought they might have forgotten that she had been in a room very near the bathroom, and then made her way to the stoep.

'Come on, Pat,' said Maggie. 'Time you had a cup of tea. You must need one. Did Podge take a long time to drop off?'

'He did a bit.' Pat sank down on to the empty chair next to Erica Scott. 'Trouble is, when he's awake, he won't stay still; he has to wander. I left the carrycot on the floor in case he wants to climb out. After all, one can't fall off the floor. I'll have to keep on going in and keeping an eye on him, though. If he *does* wake up, goodness knows where he'll end up.'

'Relax,' said Maggie. 'We'll take it in turns to go and look in on them.'

Erica turned to Pat. 'I'm told you're an old Cheltenham girl,' she said. 'You can't be very much younger than I am. We might have been there together. What house were you in?'

They discovered that they had both been day-girls, but as Cheltenham Ladies College is a very large school, and there are more day-girls than there are girls in any one other boarding house, they could quite easily have left school still strangers. Three years are endless at twelve and fifteen.

'I think I remember seeing you in the day-girls' cloakroom sometimes,' said Erica. 'Of course, I didn't finish there. I was sent out to Aunt Anna Venter in Southcliff when my parents died, not long before my sixteenth birthday.'

'Yes, I'd have been about twelve or thirteen then. The girls of fifteen and sixteen seemed impossibly grown-up.'

'One catches up. Did you know . . . ?' Patricia forgot the children in one of those fascinating 'Did you know?—Do you remember?' conversations. Looking at her indulgently, Maggie and Mary took it in turns to tiptoe into the bedroom to see if the three small boys were still sleeping. Lorraine had anexed Charles. He was a bit dull, and more interested in his—to her—rather colourless wife than in any of the other women, but he was a man, and something of a celebrity, even though his subject—natural history in general with emphasis on birds—couldn't bore her more. When he told her that a weakness in one leg, the result of an old injury, made it impossible for him to dance, she almost lost interest. She made some polite remark about being lucky to meet such a celebrity. Charles Milstead laughed.

'My sister Maggie's much better known than I am,' he said.

Lorraine looked bewildered. 'Maggie? You mean Mrs van der Berg? I didn't realise that she was your sister. I can't remember having heard her name, or the name of Maggie Milstead. I presume she's known under her maiden name, as Erica told me she and the doctor haven't been married long.'

'No, she writes for Faraday and Hopkins—romantic novels under the name of Josephine Cantrell, our mother's maiden name.'

'Oh yes, I think I have read one or two of her books.' Lorraine was wise enough not to say that she had read them when there was not much else to read, having bought them at a station bookstall. 'She goes in very much for the happy ending type of novel, doesn't she?'

'That's the thing her publishers like. Books about normal people who marry the man they want to marry.'

'And live happily ever after?' Lorraine Jorgens' voice was mocking.

'Well, everyone knows that there have got to be snags in life, but the kind of woman who reads the kind of book Maggie writes reads to forget her own troubles. She doesn't want to read about other people's—at least not really gloomy ones.'

'Personally,' Lorraine studied the toe of one impeccable shoe, 'with all respect to Mrs van der Berg, of course, I prefer something a little more realistic. I mean, how often in life does one get the happy ending?'

'More often than one might imagine, I think,' said Charles, looking across to where his wife was chatting with Maggie. 'I have, happier than I'd dared to hope at one time. Of course, anyone can make the most of life's little setbacks and make out that there's no such thing as a happy ending. Life's what you make of it. Take my wife's aunt now; she's spending Christmas with us. She was invited to spend the day with some friends on a farm, that's why she's not here with us today. She never married. I don't know how old she is; over fifty, I should think, but if Ann Burns isn't happy, I'll eat my hat.'

To Lorraine Jorgens' intense disgust, she could get nowhere near Richard that evening. While the presents were being handed down from the Christmas tree, he devoted himself entirely to the children. Afterwards, when they all sat round the big table in the dining-room for a supper of cold turkey and *hors d'œuvres* made by Maggie herself the day before, and warmed-up mince-pies which had not lost any of their crisp freshness in the process, he sat between his niece and Patricia, with every sign that he was enjoying their company.

When they were drinking coffee after the informal meal was over, she tried again.

'There's a dance at the Town Hall tonight, I believe,' she said, looking straight at Richard.

'Good lord, so there is. Want to go, Pat?'

'But the children?'

'Mary won't mind baby-sitting for you.'

'Do *you* want to go?' asked Patricia.

'Don't worry about being late, Dick,' said Maggie. 'I've got a spare key, and Paul's expecting to be called out to a confinement, so we'll probably not be locked up anyway.'

'Quite frankly,' said Richard, 'unless Pat's pining for gaiety, I'd rather run her and the kids home and join her in a nice long, cold drink of her home-made ginger-beer on the stoep, and then have an early night. Suit you, Pat?'

Pat's face glowed with delight.

'I've never heard a better idea. Quite frankly—' momentarily, her face clouded '—I had a bit of a sickener of that kind of gaiety just before my mother was killed. I'd be much happier with something quieter and simpler—like ginger-beer on the back stoep.' Dimples appeared in her cheeks.

There was an unpleasant look on Lorraine Jorgens' face as she prepared to take her leave with the Scotts. It looked as if Richard Horton was very taken with his sister's children's nanny or whatever she was. Well, she would have to play her cards carefully this time. She had lost Nicholas Shaw by being too precipitate, and by showing her hand too openly. She thought that Richard Horton would suit her far better than Nick would have done. Nick was a dedicated farmer. She thought that if she had married him, there would have been endless rows when she wanted him to take her to the towns for gay holidays, and when she wanted a new car or some new jewellery and he insisted that he needed to plough most of the money from his wool-clip back into the farm.

She remembered her sister Beryl, who had been killed in a car smash, leaving Nick a widower with a young daughter, complaining of just that. Perhaps she'd been wrong; perhaps she'd had a lucky escape when Nick had made it so plain that he preferred that niminy-piminy little girl from Scotland. An industrialist like Richard Horton, with his headquarters in town, who needed to entertain lavishly, was a much better proposition. Yes, she must go to work on Richard, but she must be careful not to antagonise him by showing how bored she was by his consideration for the girl he'd employed to look after his sister's children. Some men were funny that way. They were put off if one didn't happen to fall over a woman they happened to like. Unreasonably, she thought. But then, when Lorraine Jorgens set her sights on a man, he was not supposed to have any feelings whatsoever for any other woman, until, of course, she lost interest in him.

Patricia and Richard sat on the back stoep of Number Five, Green Street, drinking ice-cold ginger-beer in a companionable silence. An occasional cry from a night-bird cut into the continuous chirping of the crickets and the high, metallic hum of a Christmas beetle who, it seemed, did not know that the sun had set. Not far away, frogs croaked by someone's water-storage tank. Richard laughed.

'People talk about the country nights being too silent,' he said. 'Just listen to the din going on all round us.'

'It *is* quiet,' said Patricia. 'One does hear these noises in a town, at least if one doesn't live right in the city centre; then all that one hears are crickets. They're always there. But unless one's in a very quiet residential suburb, one just doesn't hear them, not to register. There's always too much night traffic. It's only because it's so quiet that we *can* listen to the night noises.'

'I suppose so. Tell me, Pat,' he tossed his glowing cigarette end out into the garden. 'It's not too quiet for you here? You don't pine for the gay lights and the bright spots?'

'Don't forget, Richard,' she said, 'the bright lights haven't very happy associations for me. Honestly, do believe me, here I'm happier than I think I've ever been in my life. I think my guardian angel must have had something to do with my being brought here.'

It never struck her as being odd that only a few months ago, she would not have given a thought to the idea that guardian angels might actually exist, let alone that she might have one who took an active part in the direction of her life.

Richard smiled to himself in the starlight.

'I'm glad to hear that, Pat, and I mean it. Well, I told Maggie I wanted an early night, so I suppose I'd better push off. You'd better come to the door with me so that you can lock up after me.'

Patricia followed Richard through the house to the front stoep and turned on the stoep light so that he could see his way down the path. Just inside the door, he turned to her.

'Thank you, Pat, for giving the children such a very happy Christmas, and all the rest of the time. You're doing a grand job.'

Putting his hands on her shoulders, he turned her to him and bent and kissed her. It was not a casual 'thank you' or 'Merry Christmas' kiss. It was a hard, strong one, and Patricia was breathless when they broke away.

'Well!' It sounded as if Richard was a little breathless too. 'Seems it's time I left. 'Night, Pat. Sleep well.'

Watching him stride down the path to the gate, and to his waiting car, Patricia realised why the idea that Lorraine Jorgens might be attracted to Richard had been so repugnant to her. It was not on his account, but on hers. She was in love with him herself, and his kiss had brought it home to her. But what chance did she have against a glamorous, sophisticated woman of the world like Lorraine?

Then, as she went slowly to bed, she remembered that she had no guarantee that Richard would prefer her even if someone like Lorraine had not turned up. There was also the fact that he had certainly not shown much sign of being attracted to her that evening. In fact—Patricia chuckled—at times, he had shown signs of what could only be termed as evasive action.

She prepared to say her prayers, a habit that she had discarded on leaving England and her grandmother, but which she had started again when she had discovered that she was expected to attend church in Blouvlei with the young Collinses. Some of it had, inevitably, rubbed off on her.

Was it right, she wondered, to pray that someone might come to love her? Was it right to pray that he would *not* love someone else?

She decided on a compromise. She prayed that if God could see His way to it, would He—could He possibly let Richard Horton fall in love with her. If, however, that was not in the plan, would it be possible to ensure that he—Richard—had a happy life.

That, she decided, was as far as one ought to go, and made things pretty safe, if her prayer for Richard's happiness was answered. She had met women of Lorraine's type in Capetown during the brief period that she had lived with her mother and stepfather before their death. She did not think anyone could be happy married to anyone like that. She climbed into bed and dropped off to sleep as soon as her head touched the pillow. That was a good thing about having three lively children to look after; whatever you might have on your mind, when you went to bed, you were far too tired to stay awake worrying about it.

CHAPTER VIII

Christmas over, life went on as it had done before. The children spent most of their time out of doors, either at home in the garden or with friends. Antoinette Verity, who had been accepted as a student nurse at her mother's old training hospital, the Jan Smuts Hospital, Southcliff, was full of it.

'I've wanted to be a nurse ever since I had my appendix out when I was fourteen,' she said, ' just before Mom and Charles got married.'

She held out her glass to Patricia, who said, ' Want some more ginger beer?'

' Love some. You know, Pat, you'd make a very good nurse.'

' Wouldn't do. I did a short time as a nurse-aide in a Capetown nursing home, but I could never get taken on to train. Haven't got the right educational qualifications. Besides, I may be all right running a house and looking after children—two or three of them—but how do you know I'd be any good with a ward full of sick people?'

' One can't, of course. Mom's a bit dubious about me, I think, but she says the only way to find out is to let me get it out of my system. By the way, are you coming out to the Scotts' place tomorrow?'

' Yes, I said to Richard that I didn't think they'd want me, and that I'd stay at home with Podge while he took the older ones, but he said Mrs Scott particularly included me in the invitation.'

' Goody!' Antoinette and Patricia had struck up a very real friendship. ' I wish that ghastly Jorgens female wasn't going to be there, though,' she added. ' None of them like her. Charles says she's still looking for another husband, and he hopes she won't get her claws into Richard.'

Patricia's heart gave a lurch, but she merely smiled.

'So far, he hasn't shown much interest in her,' she said quietly.

'He hasn't, has he? She was as mad as a snake when he got out of taking her to that dance on Christmas night. I caught a glimpse of her face. She's dangerous, Pat.'

'Yes.' Patricia spoke slowly. 'I should imagine she could be, if she was crossed in any way.'

'She has a reputation for making trouble,' went on Antoinette. 'Dad was telling Mom about it the other evening. Her sister was married to Nick Shaw who farms near Boschfontein. Beryl was just like Lorraine is, and bored stiff with farm life. Nick's old grandmother kept house for him until she got too old, then she got a distant cousin of some kind to come out from Scotland to help. Nick was just starting to fall for her when Lorraine pitched up—exactly like her sister, whom he'd fallen for, and married. Mom says that she nearly wrecked things. Some men never learn, she says. Well, Lorraine's a sticker. She didn't go even when the old lady died. It was only when she'd made things so unpleasant for Fiona—the cousin—that she ran away that Nick tumbled to what was going on. Then he threw Lorraine out, rushed off in the old farm truck to catch the train up at Cookhouse and brought Fiona home. Wasn't it romantic? Mom told Charles that she thinks Richard has too much sense of self-preservation to let himself be caught by someone like Lorraine, and besides, she's much too old for him. She must be forty at least, and he's only just over thirty.'

At that moment Mary Milstead appeared through the gap in the garden fence. She smiled at her daughter. 'Oh, there you are, dear. Pat, I just came to say that it would be a good idea if we put Podge and Pete's nappies all together in one big bag tomorrow. It would save having too much knocking about in the cars. I've got the very thing.'

She accepted the offer of tea. 'Pete's quite happy playing with Charles. I can relax for a few moments.'

'Mom,' said Antoinette, 'how long is the Jorgens woman going to park herself on Erica and Andrew?'

'It's hardly respectful to call someone so much older than yourself "the Jorgens woman",' said her mother, trying to be stern. 'Besides, how do you know they don't enjoy having her?'

'Mom!' Antoinette was thunderstruck. 'Have a heart! I know Erica and I know Andrew. Mrs Jorgens isn't their kind of person at all. I'm not a bad judge of character. I knew Charles was the right one for you as soon as I met him, remember?'

Mary laughed and relented. 'So you did. "Out of the the mouths of babes and sucklings . . ." And I happen to know, because Erica told Maggie and Maggie told me that the Scotts have decided to go away for the last week of the holidays which they hadn't been going to do, simply to get rid of Lorraine. I mean, she can hardly stay in the house when her host and hostess have gone away, can she?'

'I wouldn't put it past her,' mumbled Antoinette. 'She's got nerve enough for anything!'

'Well, Toinette, granted that you're quite right,' said Mary, 'for goodness' sake be polite to her tomorrow, even if she is rude to you.'

'She won't be rude to me, Mom,' said Antoinette. 'She doesn't waste her time being rude to anyone under twenty. She merely ignores them as she does employees. Haven't you noticed how she never speaks to Pat unless she has to, and then she's horribly condescending.'

'You're so sharp you'll cut yourself one of these days

if you're not careful,' her mother told her amiably. 'I'll take those napkins over with me and pack them now if you like, Pat. Then you'll only need a little bag with the stuff for Podge's lunch.'

Patricia grabbed Podge, who was trying to negotiate the three steps from the stoep to the garden. Carrying him on one hip, she went into the house with Mary.

They arrived, two cars full, at about half past ten. At once, Andrew Scott anexed Richard to take him and show him the performance of a 'rainbird'—the spray that is used to irrigate a large tract of ground—that he had recently bought from Horton and Verity. Charles and Antoinette, who shared one another's passion for birds, disappeared with binoculars and camera in the direction of a plantation of bluegums. Erica Scott swept Mary and Patricia up to the shaded stoep where Lorraine was decoratively arranged on a deck chair with a leg rest, showing a length of elegant leg.

'I thought the men were coming too,' she said, after greeting Mary politely and Pat briefly.

'They're here,' said Erica. 'Andrew took Richard off to look at some farm machinery that his firm supplied, and of course, Charles and Antoinette went off to look for birds. There's a family of kingfishers nesting above the dam; I don't know what kind, but Charles says they're pretty rare in these parts. I'll get Regina to bring the tea. It's a bit early, I suppose, but I think we can all do with a cup, and the others can have a fresh cup when they come if they want it, but I expect they'd rather have a long cold beer on a day life this.'

The three toddlers were put on a large rug to play where the grown-ups could keep an eye on them. Erica's Andy, being a little older and on his home ground, had to be watched in case he was too rough and overbearing with his guests. None of them had reached the age where they could be expected to give and take, or be generous in sharing favourite toys.

The two mothers and Patricia talked babies while they drank their tea, Lorraine lying languidly back in her chair and looking ineffably bored. Patricia, whose chair was by the steps that led from the stoep down to the drive, leaned forward to look at the catch of the gate that the Scotts had put there to keep little Andy from running away.

' Do you find this catch works?' she asked. 'I'm thinking of having a gate put on our stoep. I can't keep Podge in one place these days, and I'm terrified he'll stray and hurt himself. Trouble is, he's getting good at undoing catches. I think a hasp and staple and a padlock are the only things that'll keep him safe.'

Lorraine joined in the conversation at last. 'Pretty free with your employer's money, aren't you? Arranging to have fittings put on his property without a by-your-leave?'

' Dick naturally gives Pat a free hand when it concerns the safety of the children,' said Mary. 'After all, she's in sole charge when he's not here. It wouldn't be very clever of her to leave anything like that to chance.'

' Oh well, if you think it's all right. Personally, I think she's much too young to be given a responsibility like that. Still, I suppose you hold a watching brief, don't you?'

' Not exactly,' said Mary, smiling across at the discomfited Patricia. 'Dick asked me to keep an eye on things and to give Pat every help that I could until she settled down. He knew she'd feel very strange and worried, and there are lots of things where one can help —the best place to go to shop, and what they liked to eat and all that kind of thing. She learned quickly.'

' I still think she's very young for the responsibility.'

' Why?' asked Erica suddenly. 'After all, women have babies when they're in their early twenties, and they're expected to look after them in a responsible manner. I don't see why children without a mother should have to put up with a middle-aged old fogey if there's someone young and energetic enough to be a companion to them who's available, as Pat was when she was needed.'

'What about the discipline?' asked Lorraine.

At that moment Podge, who had wandered away from the other children, came to investigate the gate at the top of the steps.

'Podge,' said Patricia, 'leave that gate alone.'

Podge turned round, gave her a seraphic smile, and went on trying to open the catch of the gate.

'*Podge!*' said Patricia sternly. With another even more angelic smile, Podge went right on with what he was doing. Lorraine sneered.

'As I said,' she murmured, 'what about discipline?'

Patricia ignored her.

'PODGE!' she said, 'do you want me to get up and come to you?'

Podge wavered and looked doubtful. Patricia half rose in her chair. Podge left the gate and ran to her, squealing with delight.

'I think that answers your question,' said Mary to Lorraine. 'They not only get discipline; they appear to enjoy it!'

The rest of the day passed better than Patricia had thought. The men came back from their various ploys, and Lorraine made a dead set at Richard, who tolerated her politely enough, without showing any undue enthusiasm for her advances. Mary and Erica took Patricia under their wing, and Antoinette made no secret of the fact that she preferred Patricia's company to that of Mrs Jorgens, a fact which left Lorraine supremely indifferent. In spite of that, it seemed that Lorraine could not refrain from getting in little digs at Patricia whenever the opportunity arose. Patricia had only to open her mouth when the older woman was ready with a snub. Although the others tried to defend her, it was impossible, as Lorraine, realising that Patricia was popular with the others, was so subtle with her snubs that they were almost impossible to counter. Patricia was glad when, after tea, they piled into the two cars and were on their way back to Green Street.

Peggy and David, who had spent most of the day playing about the farm with old Sixpence, who had looked after Andrew's mother's poultry, and now did the same for Erica, had only been there for lunch and tea. They were all in Richard's car, the Milsteads having all gone in their own car which had hand controls so that Charles could manage it.

'I don't much like Mrs Jorgens, do you, Pat?' said Peggy as they turned off the rough gravel farm road, over the cattle-grid on to the main road back into Blouvlei.

'Well, I haven't known her for long enough to be able to tell,' said Pat carefully, not knowing what Richard really felt about her. 'I don't think she and I have much in common,' she added truthfully but tactfully.

'I didn't like her either,' said David. 'When I went and tried to show her the big worm we found in the garden, she said, "Go away, you horrid little boy. Is that the way that girl teaches you to behave?" What did she mean by that girl, Pat? Angelina, or Minah? Because they don't teach me how to behave, I don't have a nurse-girl. Does she think I'm a baby?'

Richard, at the wheel, made an indescribable sound, something between a snort and a laugh.

'I'm afraid she means me, David,' said Patricia. 'You see, most ladies don't like these big worms in the garden. Actually, I'm not all that fond of them myself. I'm always afraid I'll make a mistake one day, and it'll

121

be a snake, not a worm, that I meet in the garden when it's been raining.'

' You don't go on like that,' said David.

' No, that's not my way. I don't think you're a horrid little boy anyway, even if you do like wiggly worms. But don't hold it against Mrs Jorgens. Everyone doesn't like the same things.'

' And she can't help having been brought up to be rude to children. You are falling over backwards to be fair, aren't you, Pat?' said Richard.

' What do you mean?' she asked.

' Well, when you were collecting Podge's dirty napkins, Mary told me that Lorraine had been baiting you all day. She said she didn't know how you'd kept your temper.'

' Well, I couldn't very well let rip, could I?' said Patricia. ' After all, we were both Erica's guests, and it's true what she said; I am your employee. I enjoy the job, and I've made very good friends here in Blouvlei, but it's still true. Mrs Jorgens thinks I take too much on myself, by the way.'

The dark eyebrows went up. ' She does? Why's that?'

' I asked Erica if the fastening on the verandah gate was adequate, because I thought we ought to have something like it on our verandah now Podge is getting so very mobile. I never know where he's going next, and he's showing signs of being able to undo the front gate— at least he looks as though it won't be long before he can. I'll never know a peaceful moment until I've had something put up to keep him on the stoep, for he'll be climbing out of that playpen soon.

' I was looking at Erica's catch and asking if it kept Andy in as Podge seemed to be finding it easy to undo— he didn't manage it; thank goodness, he was obedient and came away when I called him. But I said that I wanted to get something put up on our verandah, and that I thought only a hasp and staple with a good strong padlock would keep Podge in when he wanted to get out, and Mrs Jorgens remarked that I was taking a good deal upon myself, being free with your money and arranging to have fittings put on your property without a by-your-leave. Is it all right if I have gates put on the verandah, Richard? It ought not to cost much, and it would be safer now that Podge walks so beautifully.'

'Of course. Look, Pat, anything you need for the good of the children, or the easier running of the house, you get. That's what you get a housekeeping allowance for. And if the C.O.L. goes up so that you find you're not managing, let me know. I'll go over things and see if there's anything that can be cut down, but I shan't be unreasonable; I'll always increase it if you can't manage. Actually, Mary says she thinks you're a very good manager. Oh, and if there's any very large item like the house needing rewiring, or the roof leaking extra badly after a big rain, you'd better let me know. After all, I can probably get it done better than you can; I know the ropes.'

'Thank you, I'll do that. Actually, it would be rather shattering if I found I had to have the place re-roofed. I'd be glad to have your advice. I wouldn't know who to get or if he was charging a fair estimate.'

Richard laughed. 'And don't worry about Lorraine Jorgens. Obviously, she doesn't understand the set-up.'

'She doesn't,' broke in Peggy. 'I heard her asking Erica when Pat was inside changing Podge's nappy if she thought it was wise, the way everyone encouraged our nanny to be so much one of the family. Erica didn't know who she meant at first, nor did I. I said we didn't have a nanny; we don't need one with you to look after things. Besides, we're too old for one, David and I.'

' And what did she say to that?' asked Richard, ignoring Patricia's horrified exclamation.

' Told me that little girls were meant to be seen and not heard, then turned round to Erica and said that was who she meant, that Pat person, she said. She wanted to know if you knew that Pat was having things done to the house without your permission, and that you spoiled us. She said it was pure chance that Podge obeyed Pat when she called him away from the gate, and that it took him a long time to decide to come, and. . . .'

' But surely she doesn't expect parade-ground obedience from a babe of less than two !' exclaimed Patricia.

' It seems that she does,' was Richard's somewhat dry answer.

' Yes, and she said to Erica that I'd got spoiled since Pat came too, interrupting grown-ups like that, and that it was time David had a good beating, frightening people with snakes.'

' That's not fair,' said David. ' I told you, it was a worm, not a snake, and anyway, what does she know about it? Pat can give beatings all right if we need them.'

Patricia's heart sank. Would Richard think she was cruel to the children? But he did not look disapproving. In fact his lips twitched and his eyebrow went up.

' And if it's not an indiscreet question, young Dave, what did you get beaten for?'

' I climbed to the top of the gum tree when old Sam, Mary's garden boy, said it wasn't safe.'

' Well, a sore tail's better than a broken neck. Perhaps you'll listen to old Sam next time,' said Richard. ' They say he's a wizard with trees; always knows what he's talking about. And I'd do what Pat says if she's such an artist with—what did you use, Pat?'

'One of his tackies.' So he was not angry and annoyed; he trusted her to chastise the children as she saw fit. Patricia heaved a sigh of relief. It was not that they were naughty children or that she took a delight in knocking them about. It was just that three very lively children did need something a little stronger than mere words when they really got the bit between their teeth.

A few days later, Mary Milstead came through the gap in the garden fence, just at teatime.

'Richard went yesterday, didn't he?' she asked.

'Yes, just after lunch.' And Patricia was missing him more than she realised she would—more than she thought possible.

'I wonder if he knew—but surely. . . . But I wonder if she knows—but she can't, or she wouldn't have stayed.'

'Sit down and have a cup of tea, Mary,' said Patricia. 'Would you like me to unlock the gate or can you climb over?'

Mary bent to examine the workmanlike lock on the low gate across the steps. 'Hmm! It'll take Podge a bit of time pick *this* lock. I'll climb over. Thanks, I'll have a cup of tea, but I mustn't stay. I just came to give you the latest bit of scandal.'

This surprised Patricia. Mary was not given to repeating scandal. 'What's happening?' she asked.

'Lorraine Jorgens isn't leaving tomorrow when the Scotts go to the sea,' said Mary.

'But she must!' Patricia stared at Mary. 'How can she stay when they've gone? You can't stay on in someone else's home when they're away unless they've invited you to stay. And somehow, I can't see Erica and Andrew Scott allowing Mrs Jorgens to make herself free of their home. I don't know them very well yet, and I know her even less, but they're not the type to invite her type to make herself at home in their house.'

'She's not staying at Applegarth,' said Mary. 'She's booked a room in the Blouvlei Hotel.'

'She hasn't! Go on, Mary, you're fooling. You've got to be joking!' Patricia was utterly incredulous.

'I only wish I was joking,' sighed Mary. 'I don't know Lorraine Jorgens much better than you do, but I do know she's man-mad. I also know that wherever she goes, she spells trouble.'

'Well, at any rate, you don't have to worry about Charles,' said Patricia. 'He's far too devoted to you.'

Mary laughed. 'I hope so; I honestly think so, but that's not the only reason I'm not worried about Charles. For one thing, although Lorraine'll be nice to him if he's the only thing in trousers in sight, she'd never really be interested in a man whose main and only interest outside his family was birds—the feathered kind, I mean. Nor would she have any interest in a man with a gammy leg. Charles, as you may have heard, had a dreadful accident a few years back. It could have crippled him. It was a bit of a miracle that he made as good a recovery as he did, but it did leave him with one weak leg. Lorraine's men have to have pots of money, like a high life, and be Mr Universe, and Charles, although he's very comfortably off, is neither.'

'I should think it would be a bit difficult for her to find a Mr Universe at her age,' said Patricia. 'I mean, I don't want to be catty, and I'm not such a child that I think anyone ten or more years older than I am is necessarily senile, but Mrs Jorgens must be round about forty, isn't she?'

'I should think so, easily,' replied Mary. 'But age wouldn't worry her if she thought she'd found the right man for her second husband, and I think she has, or at least I think she thinks she has.'

'Who's that?' asked Patricia. 'There's no one who qualifies for Mr Universe in Blouvlei. Andrew Scott is the best-looking, but he's got no eyes for anyone but Erica.'

'It's not Andrew Scott, my dear,' said Mary. 'I've an idea that she's got her sights on Richard.'

Patricia gasped. 'Richard Horton?' she breathed. '*Our* Richard?'

'Our Richard.'

'But she's too old for him!'

'My dear, she's a very well-preserved woman in her early forties. It takes money to keep as well-preserved as that.'

'Go on! Look at Maggie van der Berg. She looks much younger than that, and she's about fifty.'

'Maggie'd look younger than Lorraine at any age; she hasn't that weary-worldly, bored and blasé look that Lorraine has except when she's on the hunt and there's a nice hunk of man in the offing.'

'Well, with a daughter of Toinette's age, you can't be very far off the forties yourself, but you look a child compared to Mrs Jorgens.'

Mary gave a little mock bow. 'Thank you for those few kind words. Actually, I had a bit of a tough life until I married Charles, but my style doesn't age much, and I haven't racketed about like Lorraine has. If you live her life, you have to spend an awful lot on your appearance if you don't want to age prematurely. Anyway, she fancies herself as a glamorous woman not yet in middle-age, and as she sees him, I imagine that Dick's a dish of a man not in his first youth, with everything, looks and money, and not even a wife in the offing. She's jealous of you, my dear.'

'Of—of me? But why?'

'Because you're an attractive girl, and because Dick treats you as a human being. I think if he just threw a few instructions in your direction, and she overheard you asking humbly if he minded if you had a gate put on the verandah to keep Podge in, and if there was any sign that he kept you on a tight rein and saw that I kept an eye on you when he wasn't here, she might tolerate you. It would mean that if Richard was fool enough to marry her, they'd be kept out of her hair. You'd just be the little girl who looks after his dead sister's children, and only important because it would add to her convenience. You don't think she'd want a husband who was saddled with the responsibility of another woman's children, do you? No, if Dick treated you as the complete employee, that would suit her down to the ground.

'What gets her is that he treats you like a human being, appears to like your company, trusts you to the extent that he gives you a more or less free hand with improvements that are going to affect the welfare of the children. In short, Pat my dear, she sees in you a threat to her future with Dick.'

Patricia gaped. 'But—but that's ridiculous! I mean —Richard's nice to me; he's an absolute honey in fact, but he sees me as a child. He does seem to have a better opinion of me than he did when we first met, when he found me pretending to be Simon Verity's fiancée to get some money so that I could have a roof over my head and know where my next meal was coming from, because I was alone in the world and broke and desperate, but I'm no threat to her. I wish I was. I know he'd never look at me, but I'd rather he fell for anyone than Lorraine Jorgens. She'd never make him happy.'

'She'd never make any man happy,' said Mary. 'All I can say is, she's going to set the place by the ears if she stays long at the Blouvlei Hotel!'

'But what good does she think it's going to do her

with Richard, staying there?' asked Patricia. 'Richard doesn't live in Blouvlei. He's mostly in Southcliff, with trips to Port Elizabeth and East London, and the occasional jaunt on business to Capetown. He only comes here at odd times to see how the children are getting on and how I'm coping with them.'

'That's how clever she is,' said Mary. 'If she went and parked herself in Port Elizabeth or East London, she'd never make it with his set of friends. None of them are her type and she knows it. And she's not able to horn in on his business entertaining; she's got no right. She's no relative. She isn't even a long-standing friend who might be asked to act hostess at a dinner.

'Dick has no home but a rather impersonal little bachelor flat in Southcliff; that's his headquarters. Anywhere else, he stays at a hotel, except that he puts up at his uncle's place when he goes to Capetown. But here if anywhere, he's on his home ground. It was here that his sister lived, and he and Martha were very close. He'll always be coming back here as long as the children are here, and if she stays here, she'll be able to see him whenever he comes here, and she'll be able to make friends with his friends—she hopes. Personally, I can't see anyone here who's a friend of Dick's being particularly enamoured of her, but she could do quite a bit of damage if we let her.'

'She could? How?'

'My dear, you don't know these dorpies as I know them. I told you when you first came, if someone sneezes at one end of Blouvlei, there's a thunderstorm the other end. People talk. And how they talk! And most of the farms are on the party line and listen in to one another's conversations on the telephone. Did you ever hear how Lorraine nearly stopped Fiona Shaw's marriage to Nick, and drove her out of Boschfontein?'

'No. I did hear something of the sort, but not the

details.'

'Well, I'm not sure of the details myself, but I do know that Lorraine somehow started the whole district gossiping about poor Fiona until even Nick believed the idiotic stories that went round. Fiona was friendly with Mrs Fraser, the doctor's wife, but being stuck out in the *bundu* on the farm, she didn't go to her with her troubles until it was nearly too late.

'If Lorraine starts trying to make trouble for you, you've got Maggie and me ready to defend you, prepared for the battle before it's started.'

Patricia looked alarmed. 'D'you think there'll be a battle?' she asked. 'I'm no match for someone like Mrs Jorgens.'

'Knowing Lorraine, I should rather bet on a series of running skirmishes and a few ambushes,' said Mary, 'but don't worry; we're prepared for it. It's not as though you've got to tackle her single-handed or un-warned.' She was silent for a moment, then, suddenly, 'You love Richard, don't you, Pat?' she asked.

'Yes,' said Patricia. 'I don't expect anything to come of it. I'm years younger than he is, and not par-ticularly clever or beautiful. But he trusted me enough to give me the job of looking after his sister's children against all reason. He played his hunch; it was as simple as that. And so instead of having to scratch for a living at some dull, unskilled job, I've got a home, work I enjoy, and three darling children to look after, and he's paying me enough so that I can save, so that when the job comes to an end, when Podge is old enough not to need me any more, I'll have something to fall back on.

'Oh, I don't *want* it to come to an end, but all children grow up eventually, so I'm not fool enough to kid myself I'm here for ever. I just live in the present and enjoy what comes.

' But when Richard comes here, he doesn't go round inspecting like a policeman to see that I'm doing things the right way. No, it's do I need anything. Is everything all right or is there anything worrying you. Certainly get things you need, only let me know if it's something big like rewiring the house or needing a new roof. He treats me like a sensible human being, not an irresponsible kid he caught doing something dishonest if not illegal to get out of a tight corner. And I thought he'd be angry when David cut his leg and had to have stitches, and when Peggy got that black eye falling out of the loquat tree, but he only laughed and said he'd done the same himself at that age. Do you wonder I love him?'

' Don't worry, Pat,' said Mary, getting up to go. ' I've a feeling you'll find one another. And one thing; he enjoys your letters. Says they're the most entertaining thing he's read for years, and that you ought to be a success as a writer if ever you got an urge in that direction.'

She left Patricia looking quite dazed between apprehension about what Lorraine Jorgens could do to her future and delight because Richard enjoyed her letters.

As always when she was disturbed about something, she went to the back stoep and looked out over the garden at the quiet veld. It had so many moods; it was always the same, yet ever-changing, golden in drought, green when the rains had been good, smiling in the pitiless summer suns and dark and louring under thunder-clouds. She had come to love it as though she was born to it. Even without Richard, she never wanted to leave it, at least not permanently. This, she felt, was her home.

CHAPTER IX

Richard left for Southcliff in January the first. On New Year's Eve, there was a party at Number Three, Green Street, Charles and Mary Milstead saying that they were the only ones so far who had not offered hospitality to their friends. Patricia had said that she could not go; she must stay at home with the children. She had resigned herself to sitting and listening to sounds of revelry.

'But you must come,' said Mary. 'Bring the kids. Podge will sleep the evening out in his carrycot. Peggy'll enjoy the fun, and it won't do her any harm to sit up late for once. Our parties aren't the sort that one wouldn't want a pre-teenager to see. A few of Toinette's friends will come and dance, but they're decent youngsters. And young David will love it, and he can curl up on one of the beds when he gets sleepy.'

'Won't Richard disapprove?' asked Patricia.

'Has he ever disapproved of a little fun since you've been here?' asked Mary. 'Of course he won't. He'll say it's time you went out a bit.'

Patricia began to feel excited. A little intimate party like the one Mary described was new to her. It sounded fun, and Richard would be there. If Toinette and her friends danced, perhaps Richard would ask her to dance too.

'What does one wear?' she asked Mary, who looked vague.

'Oh, what does it matter? Something comfortable. Nothing extreme. Wear that pretty little green frock you had on at Christmas.'

So Patricia put on a leaf-green dacron frock with a softly falling shortish midi skirt, coming just to her knees, and her silver sandals. She brushed her hair until it struck gold and russet sparks where the light caught it. She wore no jewellery. All her good jewels had been sold after the crash, and she did not think costume jewellery such as she had left went with this delicate frock.

An excited Peggy in bright pink and white candy stripes, her long fair hair caught back with a pink Alice band to match, could hardly keep still. David viewed the evening with reservations. His hero, Richard, would be there, so would Charles Milstead, who knew how to talk to a chap, but there would be a lot of women there. Pat was all right, so was Mary, but most women were an awful nuisance to a man of six.

'But Maggie's all right as well as Mary,' said his sister, to whom he confided his views.

'She's all right, I suppose,' said David dubiously, 'but she's a bit *old*, isn't she? And Paul's a bit old too, although he's quite fun when he's not wanting to stick needles into one or making one take horrible medicine. Ugh! D'you remember that horrid stuff he made us take for our colds last winter? Wasn't it grotty?'

Patricia, overhearing, chuckled silently, although she felt that although they had never done it, it might have sounded better if they had said *Aunt* Mary, *Aunt* Maggie and *Uncle* Paul; Uncle Richard too, come to that. To-night, though was not the time to mention it, and as these people had allowed it long before she came on the scene, and she was only a cross between a housekeeper and a nursery governess, she felt it was no business of hers. They were wonderful people, she thought, and made her feel one of themselves nearly all the time. She was lucky to have got a job which brought her here amongst them, but there were times such as this evening, the end of the year, and the beginning of a new one, when much as she loved the place, she was conscious of being a stranger amongst them.

Patricia fastened Podge's romper and picked up a minute cardigan in case it was chilly when they came home across the garden.

' Aren't you ready, Pat?' The children came bursting into the little room next to hers, which was Podge's room.

' Just ready. Now, Podge, in you go.'

But Podge decided that he was not going into his carrycot. Every time Patricia popped him in, he climbed out.

' All right,' she said. ' If you two bring his carrycot along for when he gets sleepy, I'll bring him.' She picked him up and he wriggled until she nearly dropped him.

' Podge walk,' he said.

When Podge was in this mood, there was nothing much to be done about it. He did not cry or grizzle; he was just cheerfully determined, and thwarted all attempts to make him conform to the wishes of his elders. Patricia thought that she was not sure if he would go far or come to a sticky end, but that as a toddler, it made him, at times, infuriating.

' O.K.,' she said, taking his hand. ' You two bring the carrycot. Podge walk!'

They found the party on the back stoep, the french doors of the dining-room open to disclose a buffet table. Paul van der Berg was officiating as barman, and the guests helped themselves from the table. A glowing fire in a dry river-bed at the end of the garden, from which came shouts and cries indicated that Toinette and her friends were having a *braaivleis*.

Everyone greeted the party from next door with great friendliness—all, that is, save Lorraine Jorgens. She nodded coolly in Patricia's direction, and said in an

audible voice to Richard, who was standing by her chair:
'That girl ought not to have brought those children
here, Dick. Couldn't she have stayed at home and
looked after them? After all, isn't that what she's paid
for?'

'She's got to have some time off,' said Richard.
'Mary invited her, and she would have refused on the
children's account if Mary hadn't told her to bring them.
They're all here with my approval.'

Lorraine shrugged a beautiful bare shoulder. 'Oh,
all right, if you think it's all right. I suppose you know
your own business.'

Mary, who had sent the two elder children down to the
braaivleis at the foot of the garden, drew Patricia into
the dining-room with Podge.

'Give him some ice-cream,' she said, 'and Paul, give
Pat a drink. What's it to be, Pat?'

'Can I have a John Collins?' asked Pat.

'Surely.' Paul set about mixing it for her while Mary
fetched an outsize feeder belonging to her own toddler
and tied it round Podge.

'There,' she said, 'now he can enjoy himself, and
when he thinks he's had his share of the party, he'll
probably get sleepy and then you'll be able to have some
fun.'

'There you are, Pat,' said Paul, handing her her
drink. 'A very good drink for a hot evening.'

Pat's dimple appeared. 'I developed a liking for it in
my old unregenerate party-going days,' she said. 'One
could make it last the whole evening, so that no one
could say you had an empty glass and keep on filling
it up. There were always some people who wouldn't
believe that you didn't want another drink.'

Paul looked surprised and admiring. 'A lot of people
don't learn that lesson until they're a lot older than you
are,' he said. 'A lot never do learn it.'

'I think that was one of the things that impressed me about Pat the first time I met her,' said Richard's voice behind her. 'As far as I remember, I think I twitted her about the company she kept, and that she was a bit young for such hard drinking or something, and she showed me her glass. It was about a third full and she said that it had lasted since the beginning of the evening. That was about half past nine.'

'You'd been telling me I oughtn't to drink so much on an empty stomach, remember?' asked Patricia. 'I'd said I wanted something to eat before you interviewed me.'

'Of course. That was when my hunch began, that you might have a bit more sense than you appeared to have.'

He gave the back of her hair an affectionate tweak. 'You're looking very nice tonight. Why aren't you joining the other youngsters at the *braai*?'

'I'm waiting for Podge to get sleepy,' she said. 'He's in one of his determined moods. If he fills himself up full enough, he'll drop off, excitement or no.'

'He's thoroughly spoiled,' said Lorraine, who had come in with Richard to have her glass replenished.

'Oh, come, Lorraine,' said Richard. 'He has a pretty spartan régime usually. It's only Christmas once a year, and it is supposed to be the children's festival, isn't it?'

'Yes, darling,' said Lorraine in her brittle, affected voice, '*Christmas* is. New Year is supposed to be when the grown-ups have a chance to enjoy themselves.'

'That's just what we're trying to help Pat to do,' said Mary. 'If we hadn't invited the children, she'd have had a pretty lonely New Year's Eve, sitting next door and listening to the party, wouldn't she?'

Lorraine ignored this. She went over to where Podge was sitting at a little side table, propped up on cushions, thoroughly enjoying his treat.

'Why don't you go to sleep, little boy?' she asked: 'It's past your bedtime.'

Podge looked up from his ice-cream, and it was only too evident that he strongly disapproved of Lorraine.

'Go 'way!' he said sternly, lifting a spoon full of ice-cream. Lorraine only just removed herself from the line of fire in time.

'Oh, Podge!' wailed Patricia. 'Mary, look at your carpet!'

Mary laughed. 'Don't worry, it's not a good one. Don't forget, I've a toddler of my own.'

'It's as I said,' said Lorraine furiously as she swept out. 'Spoiled rotten!'

Mary went across and kissed Podge heartily on the cheek.

'I know just how you feel, sweetheart,' she said.

Podge merely blew bubbles with his ice-cream.

'By the way,' Mary asked Patricia, 'why do you use that big pram when you take Podge down town with you? His pushcart would be lighter, and it's very hot walking at this time of the year.'

'It's handier for the shopping,' said Patricia. 'You can't get everything sent. I'm always having to bring back shoes that have been mended and that kind of thing.'

'What you want is a car,' said Richard. 'Do you drive, Pat?'

'Yes, why?' She had not been listening properly, half her attention being on Podge, ready to prevent more ice-cream going on the carpet.

'Had much experience of driving?'

'I used to drive Mummy's Mini in Capetown. Of course, that was sold.'

'If you can drive in Capetown traffic, you can drive anywhere,' said Richard. 'Right. You get a Mini to do the shopping as soon as I can get one delivered after the holiday.'

'Is she to be allowed private mileage?' asked Lorraine, who had come back to see what was keeping Richard.

'What on earth do you mean?' Patricia felt that she would have shrivelled up and died had Richard looked at her the way he was looking at Lorraine. She had hated the idea that the older woman might manage to ensnare him, but now, although it looked as though the opposite was true, Patricia felt uncomfortable. This was spoiling the pleasant atmosphere in which she had been living since she came to Blouvlei.

Lorraine, however, appeared to notice nothing amiss.

'I mean that Miss Lang has very little supervision at her job,' she said. 'What's to prevent her from gadding about in a car that's given her for use on the job? You ought to make her submit an account of petrol and mileage if you're going to be so foolish as to let her have the use of a car.'

'Don't be so silly, Lorraine,' said Richard. 'Pat's an individual, doing a job for the family, not an employee of the firm. I wouldn't insult her by asking for a petrol and mileage log.'

'I hope you know what you're doing,' said Lorraine.

'I think so,' said Richard. 'I don't think you need concern yourself with my handling of my own family affairs.'

This time Lorraine appeared to get the message. Once more she shrugged, and looking annoyed, went out and started to talk to Charles Milstead. Richard followed her at some distance, looking thoughtful.

Patricia picked up the now sleepy Podge, and Mary came with her into the bedroom where the carrycot had been placed on the floor beside young Peter Milstead's cot.

'Come on, Pete,' said Mary. 'High time you were potted. Pat, there's another pottie in that cupboard if you think Podge ought to have attention.'

Both babes obliged, more asleep than awake, and were put down to sleep. Podge, remarked Patricia, had forgotten about his sleepy-time bottle.

'I'm hoping to break him of it eventually,' she said, 'but one doesn't want to do it too abruptly. If he hadn't started it because he was missing his parents, I'd be tougher about it, but I don't want to bring that time back for him. One doesn't know how much babies of his age remember.'

'Where did you learn all this about children, Pat?' asked Mary.

'Partly from my Aunt Gwennie,' said Patricia. 'She lived next door to Granny, and I was always having to go in and help her. She didn't have a clue about children. I suppose still being one myself, I knew what made them tick, and a lot of it stuck. And I've been getting books on child care and child psychology since I've been looking after these three.'

'You *have* been doing the job thoroughly,' said Mary, admiration and respect in her voice.

'Yes, well, you see, I just couldn't get over the way Richard had decided to trust me against all appearances. It made me determined not to let him down. And of course, I knew a bit what the children must have felt like from my own experience. Not that the books helped much. The children haven't acted as though they were particularly bereaved or deprived. I suppose they got over the worst of it when they were staying with you. The only real sign is Podge's nightly bottle.'

'Well, Podge, apart from disapproving of having someone different to put him to bed at night, was too young to know what had happened,' said Mary. 'The other two were more difficult, but I managed to help them to get over the hardest part with a series of treats. Really, it's a wonder that they've settled down to a routine with you as well as they have done. I think it says a lot for the wise way in which you've handled them.'

Patricia laughed. ' I think it's almost as much because I'm young,' she said. ' They told me they'd been terrified they were going to get someone like Mrs Browning, the Matron of the junior girls' hostel at the school.'

' Come on,' said Mary. ' These two will sleep for hours. Let's go and enjoy ourselves.'

Peggy had come up the garden as they emerged on to the stoep.

' Come on, Froggy,' she said. ' We've saved some *braai* for you.'

She seized Patricia's hand and dragged her down the garden to the wood fire in the old dry river bed, where the younger guests were cooking meat over an open fire, spearing it on sharpened sticks. They all greeted Patricia with enthusiasm, for she was popular with the younger fry of Blouvlei. They said she was a good sport for a grown-up and did not put on side.

Although she would have liked to stay near Richard, she was happier down here with people nearer her own age, and away from Lorraine Jorgens' barbed tongue.

Later, the younger and most of the older members of the party joined and danced in the dining-room to the music of a record-player.

' Come along, Charles,' said Lorraine, who could never leave well alone, and who was still annoyed with Richard for his championship of Patricia. ' Let's do this one.'

Charles remained firmly in his chair. ' Sorry, Lorraine, I don't dance.'

' But this isn't one of those modern jive, beat and that sort of thing. It's a slow foxtrot.'

' I'm sorry,' said Charles blandly. ' I just don't dance.'

' Oh, come on, be a sport.'

'Sorry, Lorraine, it's out of the question.'

'Oh, Charles, why won't you?'

'Because it isn't possible.'

'Don't be stupid! You're just being rude and idiotic!'

Lorraine was becoming angry. Paul van der Berg intervened.

'He's not being stupid or rude, Lorraine,' he said. 'He's just using his common sense.'

Lorraine whipped round. So far, she had more or less ignored Paul van der Berg. To her, he was just a dull country G.P., too old and too obviously devoted to his wife to be interesting.

'You—what do you mean?' she snapped.

'Surely you've heard about Charles's accident?' asked Paul. 'It was only about three years ago that he got properly on to his feet again. For a long time he was in a wheelchair, and then on crutches with walking calipers and a spinal brace. Before that, there were painful operations and long convalescence. He's still got a weak leg that could let him down if he does anything silly. Just leave him alone, will you? Use a little tact.'

Charles grinned. 'It's all right, Paul, I know Lorraine's type. She reminds me of Joyce Caraday.' He winked at Mary. 'Remember that time she stayed here and Maggie was so mad with her because she tried to make Toinette and you share that tiny bedroom?'

Mary laughed. 'Do I not! How that girl hated me. It was a long time before I realised that it was a compliment that she regarded me as a rival.'

They might have been alone together in the room. Patricia envied them their unity. This was what a marriage ought to be.

'How do you come to know Joyce Caraday?' asked Lorraine curiously. 'She's my cousin.'

'Oh, so that's why she reminds me of you—at least you remind me of her,' said Charles. 'As a matter of fact, she and I met at art school in Capetown. We got engaged, but after my accident, when it was thought that I might be permanently crippled, I offered her her freedom. Although I was relieved that there was no argument—I couldn't have taken tears and that kind of thing just then—it didn't do much for my self-esteem when she accepted it eagerly, and got engaged to someone else within a fortnight.

'Of course, the poor girl had a thing about bodily deformity. She didn't come near me in hospital until she'd been assured that my face wasn't disfigured. She pitched up here when Mary was still nursing Dad and me. I suppose she'd heard a rumour that I was more or less on my feet again, and her second engagement had fizzled out. She tried to get me back again, but I'd already fallen in love with Mary, although I hadn't admitted it.

'Yes,' he went on slowly. 'In some ways, you and Joyce are very much alike. The only real difference is that Joyce is a bit of a puritan and you, my dear Lorraine, are anything but that!'

'Charles,' said Lorraine, controlling her temper with an effort, 'you know, you're being rather nasty, aren't you?'

'Of course,' said Charles. 'I'm rather a nasty person. Didn't you know?'

'Charles,' said his wife, 'behave yourself, darling. You're as bad as Toinette.'

She said it humorously and lovingly and the whole crowd laughed and the moment of tension passed. As soon as she could do it without seeming obvious, Lorraine pleaded a headache.

'One of my migraines coming on,' she said. 'Richard, please run me down to the hotel?'

'Shame, do you feel a bit under the weather?' asked Richard with off-hand sympathy. 'All right, Lorraine,

I'll be glad to. All right, Mary, I'll be back in time to see the New Year in.'

At five minutes to twelve, Patricia was standing half hidden by the curtain, just inside the dining-room french doors. She had not heard the little episode when Charles and Lorraine had crossed verbal swords, having been taking her turn at going to see if the toddlers were sleeping, and at the same time tucking David, who had had more than enough party, on one of the beds until they were ready to go home.

Someone had mentioned in passing that Richard had taken Lorraine back to the hotel because she had felt a migraine coming on, but had given no details.

Somehow, Patricia had managed to hide her disappointment, but at the first opportunity had managed to escape from the crowd, and was now gazing wistfully out into the star-spangled night. She was sorry if Lorraine was not feeling well, but it was just like her, thought Patricia, to spoil everything. Patricia had set such store by this party. She had hoped for at least one dance with Richard. Surely that wasn't too much to ask for? And she had thought that they would be seeing the New Year in together.

She blinked fiercely as the stars swam together. She simply must not cry. It would make her look ridiculous, and it would spoil things for everyone else. If they noticed, they would be sure to ask what was the matter, and she could not tell them. There would be no excuse that she could make that would hold water either. You couldn't have two of the female guests at a New Year party pleading a headache; it would stretch credibility too far.

A dark figure strode lightly up the steps as the clock struck twelve. Pat slipped further behind the curtain.

'Dick!' cried Mary. 'Just in time to be the first-footer!' Mary's ancestors had been Scottish. She had been Mary Gordon before she had married Tony Verity.

'I told you I'd be back,' said Richard. 'Happy New Year, everyone. Come on, Pat, what are you doing, hiding behind the curtain?'

He took her hand and pulled her out, and taking her in his arms, kissed her heartily.

'A very Happy New Year, Patricia,' he said.

This was the signal for a perfect orgy of kissing and good wishes. Patricia thought that Charles kissed her twice. Paul kissed her once, very heartily and kindly, and she was sure that Richard kissed her three times before they all formed a ring for the singing of *Auld Lang Syne*.

It was Richard's hand that held hers while they sang the sentimental but poignant old song. It was Richard who, when the song was over, swept her on to the floor when Toinette put on a record for more dancing.

It was a waltz, an old Deanna Durbin number—*Waltzing in the Clouds*. It expressed perfectly the way Patricia felt.

'Enjoying yourself?' asked Richard, smiling down at her happy face.

'It's perfect,' she said. 'I thought you weren't coming back.'

'But you heard me tell Mary I'd be back when I'd taken Lorraine down to the hotel.'

'I wasn't in here then. I'd taken David to lie down; he'd had enough. And I went to see if Podge and Peter were all right.'

'So you missed all the fun?'

'Fun?'

'When Lorraine tried to get Charles to dance.'

'No, I was here then. I was impressed; it suddenly struck me what a very united couple Charles and Mary are.'

'They're a grand couple. I'm glad you've got them for neighbours, Pat. They see that you don't overwork, don't they?'

Patricia laughed. 'They're always trying to get me to go out and play,' she said. 'I can't leave the children *all* the time. Besides, they're fun—the children, I mean.'

'So you don't regret taking on the job?'

'Regret it? It was the best thing I ever did!'

Richard laughed at her earnestness, and clasped her more firmly around the waist as he whirled her about the Milsteads' dining-room.

It was not long after that that the party broke up. Mary and Patricia made tea and coffee, giving everyone the choice.

'Not a very good nightcap, Mary,' said Paul. 'None of us will have any sleep, drinking stimulants at this hour.'

'Rubbish, Paul,' said his wife. 'I often have a cup of tea before turning in, and I always sleep well enough.'

Patricia took a little time to get to sleep. She did not know when she had been so happy, but a little warning bell rang at the back of her mind. It told her that she must not take it too seriously that Richard had kissed her Happy New Year before he had kissed the others. It was simply that he had spotted her behind the curtain, and that she was nearest to him when the clock struck twelve.

She must not set too much store by the fact that he had held her so closely and had smiled down at her as he had done while they were dancing to *Waltzing in the Clouds*. It would be too utterly childish and ridiculous to read anything into the events of a light-hearted New Year party, although she was glad that he did not seem to be taking Lorraine Jorgens' advances too seriously.

In spite of her sternness with her dreams, her waking dreams, at any rate, once she was asleep, she could no longer control those dreams. For what remained of the night, she was whirling amongst the stars, Richard's arm about her and his bright hazel eyes laughing down into hers.

CHAPTER X

At the beginning of February, Antoinette Verity left to
begin her nurse's training. The night before she left
home, she went next door to Number Five to say goodbye to the Collins children and Patricia.

'We'll miss you, Toinette,' said Patricia.

'I'll miss all of you too, but I'm so looking forward
to it,' said Antoinette,' 'although I'm a bit scared too,
in spite of knowing a bit about it from what Mom's told
me.'

'I suppose it's only natural,' said Patricia. 'One's
always a bit scared of starting something new. I know
I was terrified when I was coming here.'

Peggy let out a hoot of laughter. 'Get away, Pat!
You were never scared of coming *here*?'

'How did I know what you'd be like?' asked Patricia.
'You were afraid of getting someone like Mrs Browning,
remember?'

'So we were.' Peggy's mind went off at a tangent.
'Toinette, you simply *must* get home for our school
sports.'

Antoinette looked doubtful. 'I'll try, Peg-top, but
I don't know if I'll be able to make it. After all, I'm
not likely to be given a long weekend off during my very
first month, and it's a job to get up here and back in
the time unless one manages to get a lift.'

'Oh!' Peggy pouted. 'You've always missed them
before because you've been away at school. I did think
you'd be able to come now you've left. Couldn't you
start a month later?'

'I don't really know. Matron said February the first.
I don't think she'd like it if I wanted to put it off for a
months, unless it was for something like illness or some-

thing like that. I'll try to come, Pegs, but I can't promise.'

Peggy was a sensible child, so she stopped trying to persuade Antoinette to get the time off. Instead, she said, ' D'you think Dick will be able to come?'

' I don't know, Peggy.' Patricia felt herself turning a little pink. ' I'm sure he would if he isn't too busy.'

' Are you going to write and let him know?'

' I—I hardly think—well, I'll mention it next time I write.' Patricia still wrote long progress reports to Richard, and would have been most embarrassed as well as highly delighted had she known how much he enjoyed reading them.

' Why don't you write and ask him if he can get away, Peggy?' she asked.

' I think that's a good idea.' Antoinette backed Patricia up. ' After all, it's your school sports.'

' And my birthday. Dick *must* come for my birthday, Pat. Oh, I do hope he won't be tied up with some tiresome business.'

' I'm sure he'll come if he can, Peg-top,' said Antoinette. ' He's far too fond of both of you to miss either of your birthdays.'

' Aren't I lucky?' said Peggy. ' Me being eleven on the very day of the sports means that I'm illegible to run in the under-eleven race.'

Patricia and Antoinette smiled at one another behind Peggy's back.

' I think the word you want is " eligible ",' said Patricia gently.

' Of course. I always muddle them up."

Antoinette left soon. She did not want to be away from her mother for too long on her last evening at home, and she still had some last-minute packing to do. She must not be too late to bed the night before the great day.

148

Peggy fetched pad and envelopes and composed a careful letter to her Uncle Richard, stating exactly why he would enjoy her school sports as well as its being her birthday.

Patricia ran into Lorraine Jorgens in the dorp the next day. She was buying new shorts for Peggy who, although not a tall child, was shooting up lately.

'One can't find a thing worth wearing in the shops here, can one?' she drawled.

Patricia, who had bought several tub frocks to wear about the house, her old Capetown wardrobe being, although good, a little unsuitable for wear about the house while caring for two children, murmured something non-committal.

Lorraine looked down at Podge in his pushcart.

'Isn't it a dreadful nuisance, trailing that child around with you everywhere?' she asked. 'Why don't you leave him at home with the girl when you come shopping? Then you could use the car.'

Richard, true to his promise, had bought a Mini which he had had insured in Patricia's name, and had given her the use of it.

'I did come down in the car,' replied Patricia. 'Podge's pushcart folds up and goes in the boot. There's a little sort of hanging chair thing that fixes on to the seat and he's strapped in so that he doesn't fall forward and hurt himself when I brake.'

'More expense for poor Dick!' Lorraine looked down her nose.

'*I* didn't buy it on the expense account!' Patricia was stung into self-defence. 'Richard bought it himself last time he was here.'

'Oh!' With that flat little monosyllable, Lorraine swept out, leaving Patricia feeling ruffled and annoyed. Normally, she thoroughly enjoyed these shopping expeditions. Somehow Lorraine Jorgens seemed to have the power to spoil everything with which she came into contact.

Her purchases done, she took Podge into the café, having promised him an ice-cream if he was good. She thought she deserved one herself. In the café, she found Erica Scott sitting on her own.

'Come and join me. Hello, Podge; you grow a bit every time I see you.'

Erica was in the seventh heaven. She had been to see the doctor who had confirmed the fact that she was expecting another baby. 'But don't say a word. I haven't told Andrew yet. That'll put paid to Lorraine Jorgens chasing him!' She sipped her coffee happily.

'But she didn't chase Andrew, did she?' Patricia could not believe it.

'Women like that chase anything in trousers,' said Erica, 'not that she got anywhere with Andrew, but it becomes tedious. He was always having to race for cover. I wish she'd go back to Capetown where she belongs.'

'Does she? I never knew she came from there.'

'She was married to a Capetown businessman, and when she was waiting for the divorce to come through, she went and stayed with her brother-in-law in the Boschfontein District until the scandal died down. Of course, she could never do anything without making a stir. She turned Boschfontein upside down. We told you about that, didn't we? When she nearly wrecked Nick's chance of a happy second marriage? She went back to Capetown for a while after that, then she came back and parked herself on us. Andrew's a sort of distant cousin, didn't someone tell you? Everywhere she goes, sooner or later she makes the place too hot to hold her and goes somewhere else to cause a scandal while she waits for the first one to die down.

Honestly, Pat, I'm not normally catty, but that woman—! I thought I'd met some types while I was nursing, but she beats the lot!'

Richard promised to be in Blouvlei by lunchtime on Friday, so he would be there to see the finals of Peggy's race. She prayed that she would reach the finals, as she was only competing in the one event, the under-eleven seventy-five-metre race. The heats were run off at intervals all day, so as Patricia could not leave in the morning, a heated Peggy kept appearing at home for cool drinks or to change into a clean pair of shorts.

'The finals are being run off at three,' she said to Patricia as she ate a hasty lunch.

'I wish you'd wait and rest a bit,' said Patricia. 'You're so hot and sweaty.'

'But they may want me to run in another heat at any time, Pat,' protested Peggy. 'And I don't want to miss a moment of it. It's all so fun. Oh, I *do* hope Richard gets here in time for the finals!'

It seemed to Patricia that Peggy was far too sure of reaching the finals. True, she was running in the semi-finals, but anything could happen, and there were some much taller girls running, even though Peggy was at the top of her age-group. She tried to tell Peggy this, but the child brushed away her remarks.

'Oh, none of them are very fast, Pat. If I don't get into the finals, I ought to be ashamed of myself!'

The school was only just round the corner, in easy walking distance, so Patricia had not intended to go by car. At half-past two, she deposited Podge with Mary Milstead, who was going to put him for his afternoon rest with her own little boy. She was just coming out of the gate of Number Three when Richard's car drew up outside Number Five, and Richard's head poked out of the driver's seat window.

'Going to the sports?' Come on!' he called. Patricia ran up to the car, expecting to be sitting beside him, but had to climb into the back as Lorraine Jorgens was sitting in the front passenger seat. Patricia hoped that she managed to hide the fact that she was taken aback as she greeted the older woman. What on earth was Mrs Jorgens doing, going to see the school sports of a school in a small backveld dorp, even though the school was quite a large and noted boarding school, and even though, being a combined affair, the girls, juniors and seniors all taking part as well as the boys.

Lorraine was the acme of smartness, in what was obviously a model suit, in light maize with a slim midi skirt. It would be far too hot to wear in the bright February sunshine, and the enormous picture hat that she wore would be a dreadful nuisance, Pat thought, in the crowded grandstand. Pat herself was dressed in one of her favourite cool dacron frocks with a skirt long enough—just below the knees—and wide enough for comfort. As they would be under cover on the grandstand, she had not bothered with a hat, but had put a pair of dark glasses in her handbag in case the glare was bad.

The grandstand was crowded, and they had to climb a good way up and then walk over people's legs before they could find three seats together. Patricia could not think why Lorraine had come. Quite obviously, she was not enjoying herself. Children of all shapes, ages and sizes were clambering up and down, sucking ice-creams and lollipops, and drinking cool drinks out of bottles through straws, looking for parents and friends. The noise was indescribable. Everyone yelled for his or her particular team all the time a race was being run, and whenever a race ended, it did not seem to matter who won, everyone raised both arms above their heads and cheered, 'Yay! Yay!' at the tops of their voices.

David found them first.

'I was beaten in the under-eights,' he told them cheerfully. 'I'm glad. Now I can spend the rest of the time having ice-creams with Tommy and Piet van Staden.'

Patricia laughed. 'Don't make yourself sick, will you?' she said. Richard fished in his pocket and brought out a twenty-cent piece which he handed to his nephew.

'*Thank* you, Dick,' said David fervently. 'Now I can beat Tommy. He said I couldn't eat more ice-creams than he could. I said I could if I had enough money for them. Now I have. 'Bye now.'

Lorraine looked down her nose in a characteristic way. Patricia and Richard both laughed.

'Looks as if you'd have done better to buy him a packet of bicarbonate of soda,' remarked Patricia.

'Yes, but he wouldn't have appreciated it half so much,' replied Richard.

'Yes, and *you* won't be the one to cope if he's sick tonight,' was Patricia's laughing rejoinder.

Peggy found them then, clambering over Lorraine's light suit, to her annoyance.

'Look out; you're making me all dirty!' she said crossly.

'Sorry, Mrs Jorgens. Oh, Dick, I'm so glad you got here in time! The finals are being run at half past three!' she exclaimed.

'Half past? I thought it was three o'clock!' Patricia was dismayed. She was afraid that if Lorraine became restive, as she showed every sign of doing, Richard would be prevailed upon to leave before Peggy ran in the Finals.

For herself, although it was hot, dusty and noisy, she thought that she could sit there all the afternoon quite happily. In spite of the turmoil made by the yelling, excited children, and the noise of the tannoy announcing events or giving out the winners, there was an under-lying sense of peace. The white clothes of the competi-tors against the green turf of the sports field, the back-ground of hills behind, gold in the bright summer afternoon sun, with the mountain deep blue to one side, over all the hard blue sky, dotted about with one or two dazzling white clouds and shading to pastel pinks and mauves in the distance as the sun sank held her eyes quite as much as the children did.

It was all a perfect setting for the school, a rambling cream-washed building decorated with the traditional ornamental gables under red-tiled roofs, with later additions harmonising well looked as if it had been there for ever. It was new by the standards that Patricia had known. Even her own old school in Cheltenham, though it was of Victorian origin, seemed to have weathered with time until its Cotswold stone arches might have been mediaeval. This was about seventy years old—a good age in the history of the Eastern Cape —but it had its traditions, and it was a fitting home for them.

She was gazing dreamily at the mountain, darkening as the sun became lower, when Lorraine broke into her thoughts.

' When's this race coming off?' she asked impatiently. ' I thought Peggy said it was to be run at half past three.'

' Oh, they announced just now that it was being put back until after the relay races,' said Richard. ' Didn't you hear?'

Lorraine shrugged her shoulders discontentedly. ' I wish they'd get a move on, then we could go somewhere comfortable.'

Richard smiled to himself and said nothing. Patricia was afraid that Lorraine might prevail upon Richard to leave before the prize-giving ceremony. It was by no means a foregone conclusion that Peggy would win her finals, but if she did, she would be terribly disappointed if Richard was not there to see her go up and receive her cup.

The relay races seemed to take for ever. They were run all the way round the perimeter of the field, and were less exciting than the shorter races, as it was difficult to see the runners on the far side of the field. The girls ran first, looking hot in their track suits, then the boys. At last they were over, to the inevitable accompaniment of the cheers: 'Yay! Yaaay!'

The half dozen little girls in the finals of Peggy's race lined up immediately opposite the grandstand.

'Ooh! Thank goodness we'll have a good view,' breathed Patricia. Richard smiled.

'I believe you're really excited,' said Lorraine.

'Of course I am!' exclaimed Patricia.

'Funny child!' said Lorraine with condescending indulgence, making Patricia writhe inwardly.

The starter's pistol went, and they were away. At first, it seemed as if Peggy was not going to be anywhere near the front. Then, slowly, agonisingly slowly, it seemed, she drew ahead, passing a thin girl who was much taller than she was and a beefy child who looked as if she could keep on for ever.

'That hefty child would be better for cross-country running than for sprints like this,' murmured Richard.

Then Peggy was in front, running before them all, and then she was across the tape—first.

'*Yaay*, YAAAY!' yelled all her excited friends. Everyone seemed to be her friend or supporter. The children were so excited that they were now cheering everyone and anyone. Patricia, a suspicious lump in her throat, found that she was clutching Richard's hand. He had been shouting, 'Come on, come on, Peggy!' as loudly and with as much excitement as any of the children. Patricia had been silent, and now it felt as though she had been holding her breath all through the race.

A hot, damp, flushed Peggy clambered up the grand-stand for their congratulations. She flung herself across Lorraine and into Richard's arms.

'Mind my *dress*!' exclaimed Lorraine irritably, but no one heard her.

'Well done, young Peg!' Richard kissed his niece and gave her a hearty congratulatory slap on the rear. Patricia flung her arms round Peggy.

'Oh, Pegs, it was wonderful,' she said. 'If I wasn't shouting it was because I was too excited to breathe! Congratulations, love. I haven't been so thrilled for years!'

Lorraine began to get up, collecting her handbag and settling her picture hat more securely on her head.

'Well,' she said, 'now that all the excitement's over, we can go and find somewhere more comfortable to sit.'

Peggy's face fell.

'But aren't you going to wait and see me get my cup?' she asked.

'Of course we are,' said Richard. 'If you've got an appointment, Lorraine, I'm sure you'll be able to find someone to give you a lift back to the hotel. People are coming and going all the time.'

'But you've watched Peggy win her race. Isn't that what we came for?'

'I believe in doing the job properly. I'm waiting to see her go up to get her cup.'

Patricia could have kissed him, right there in front of everyone.

'When will that be?' asked Lorraine.

Richard consulted his programme. 'Oh, in about another half-hour, I should think.'

Lorraine consulted her diamond-studded wrist-watch, and subsided sulkily on to the hard seat. It was half past four.

In fact, the prizegiving was at nearly half past five. The sun had still a long way to go before it set, but the shadows were lengthening, the distant mountains were darker, and a mellow golden light lay on everything. The pastel shades on the horizon were wider, sweet-pea colours of palest mauve, pink and blue. The shadow cast by the shelter which held the important people, the headmaster, the principal of the girls' school, members of the school board and the wife of the member of the provincial council who had consented to come and present the prizes, nearly reached the grandstand.

At last the final race was run, some of the children and a good many of the parents had left. All those who had won prizes were sitting in a white-clad group on the grass in front of the shelter.

It seemed an age before Peggy's name was called. First were the senior events, the competitors big girls and boys of sixteen and seventeen. At last it was the turn of the little ones. A blushing Peggy went up to receive her cup amidst clapping and cheers. Even then she could not join them, but had to wait until the little group of winners was dispersed, all the cups and shields presented.

The crowd began to leave the grandstand, Richard and the two women with them. Parents and offspring met at the foot of the steps. Lorraine, who loathed being buffeted, turned irritably to Richard.

' I don't see why we couldn't have started to leave before the crush,' she said. ' After all, we'd seen Peggy get her cup. That was what you wanted, wasn't it?'

' If we'd tried to get away in the middle of the prize-giving,' said Richard, ' we'd have got in the light of all the parents who were trying to see *their* offspring go up for their prizes.'

Lorraine shrugged and went on ahead.

Peggy was waiting for them at the foot of the grandstand steps.

'I didn't try to come up and meet you,' she explained. 'It would have been an awful job to get to you with everyone coming down, and I knew you'd be here soon.'

'Very wise,' said Richard gravely. 'Where's David?'

Peggy looked round. 'He said he'd be here. I don't know. Last time I saw him, he was sitting in front of the grandstand, eating ice-cream with Tommy van Staden. I think he was winning.'

'And the only prize for that, presumably, is a tummy-ache,' said Richard. 'Come on, let's look for him. It sounds as though your remedy will be needed tonight, Pat.'

'A few ice-creams won't make David sick,' said Peggy scornfully. 'He's tough!'

David, discovered sitting on the grass in front of the grandstand, eating ice-cream in company with a young man as grubby as he was himself, certainly appeared perfectly happy and healthy.

'Hello, is it time to go home?' he asked.

'High time. Come on, young man.' Richard waited, perfectly patiently for David to say goodbye to his friend, which entailed a good deal of, 'See you tomorrow,' and 'Remember you know what,' until Patricia grabbed him by the elbow.

'Come *on*, Dave. We're all waiting for you. We want to get home if you don't!' she said, pulling him firmly away.

Lorraine, who had gone on ahead, was waiting impatiently for Richard to come and unlock. When he drew up outside the hotel for her to leave, she said, 'No, Dick. We'll drop the children first.'

Pat felt a little icy shock of surprise. She had thought that Lorraine regarded her as a not very superior servant, but it appeared that she was classed as one of the children. It was well known that Lorraine was not fond of children.

'But I'm having supper with them,' said Richard.

'You're what? But you never said . . .'

'I never said anything, Lorraine. I'm sorry if you misunderstood, but I never made any arrangement with you for tonight. Of course I must have supper with Peggy on her birthday.' Richard sounded quite firm on this subject.

'But they said . . . isn't her party tomorrow because of the sports?' For once, Lorraine appeared to be slightly put out of countenance.

'So it is, but that doesn't stop me from eating with her tonight as well, does it? You can come up with us to Green Street if you want to, Lorraine, but it seems a bit of a waste of time, seeing that it'll mean my bringing you back and then going straight back to Green Street.'

Lorraine gave one of her scornful shrugs and climbed out of the car with an ill grace. Immediately, Richard put a large hand over to the back and hauled Peggy into the front of the car.

'Come on, birthday girl,' he said. 'The front of the car's your place today.'

Peggy was crimson with delight, then a thought struck her.

'Dick, you *are* coming to my party tomorrow, aren't you?'

'Of course, Pegs. Why not?'

'Well, I wondered if, seeing that you're coming to supper tonight . . .'

'You heard me say to Mrs Jorgens that there was nothing to stop me from having supper with you tonight *as well*, didn't you, juggins?' said Richard affectionately.

'I hope you don't mind, it's only cold,' said Patricia from the back seat.

'Why should I mind cold supper when I've got two pretty girls to eat it with as well as the champion ice-cream eater of the district?' asked Richard.

Patricia glowed quietly to herself. Richard might never see her as anything but the waif that he had rescued and put to look after his niece and nephews, but she would have hated him to succumb to Lorraine. She would rather see him marry almost anyone else who would make him happy. She was sure that Lorraine would never do that.

This evening, it was obvious that he had no intention of dancing to Lorraine's piping. Looking back, Patricia remembered many little incidents that should have told her this, but she had been blinded by Lorraine's persistence and sophistication, as well as by Richard's unfailing politeness. This evening he had, still politely, snubbed her thoroughly by showing her that he would rather be with someone else.

Patricia shivered suddenly. Lorraine would not take kindly to being turned down for three children and a nursery-governess-cum-housekeeper, even if the three children were his niece and nephews; even though one of them had a birthday that day. And Lorraine was a vindictive woman. One only had to look at that pointed, foxy little face to realise that fact.

Firmly Patricia thrust the thought of Lorraine from her mind, and prepared to enjoy the evening that Richard was to share.

CHAPTER XI

Peggy's birthday party took the form of an al-fresco afternoon meal in the garden. It could not be called 'tea' as the great majority of the guests drank highly coloured mineral water out of the bottle, through straws. The cake, baked by Minah and iced by Peggy, was placed in the middle of the groundsheet on which the guests sat, and the eleven candles, lit before it was borne out by a smiling Minah, hardly wavered in the still afternoon.

Both Milsteads were there with their little boy, who joined Podge in some obscure game of their own. A deck chair was placed for Charles, who because of his accident of several years ago found it difficult to sit on the ground, and once there, almost impossible to get up again. Mary and Charles, in common with most of the guests, brought their small gifts for Peggy. Richard's gift, a new bicycle, had been presented that morning. He arrived rather late at the party, and Peggy insisted upon waiting for him before they brought out the candle-lit cake. By the time he did arrive, she was becoming worried, and some of the younger guests impatient to know when they could eat.

He arrived with Lorraine Jorgens in tow.

Both Peggy and Patricia were aghast. Neither of them liked Mrs Jorgens, and she certainly was the last person to fit in with the crowd at an eleven-year-old's birthday party. She followed Richard out into the garden, and when he sat down with the others on the groundsheet, she hung about by Charles Milstead's chair.

Charles, after greeting her politely, but without enthusiasm, asked, 'What's the matter, Lorraine? You look a bit disconcerted.'

'Don't be silly, Charles. I can't squat down there like a child, even if Rick forgets his age.' Lorraine sounded irritable.

'I don't see why not. Even if you're older than you look, you're slim and supple enough. And you're wearing pants, not a skirt, so you've nothing to worry about there.'

Lorraine looked down at her perfectly tailored pale blue trouser-suit.

'That's just it,' she said. 'What would this look like after I'd been sprawling about on a groundsheet where a lot of children had been running around with dirty feet?'

'Moral,' said Charles, 'come suitably dressed if you want to enjoy a party.'

'But when Dick said it was Peggy's birthday tea, I thought we'd be sitting round a table.'

'And we're not. I'm the only one expected to need a chair, because everyone knows that once down, it's all but impossible to get me up again. Everyone else is thoroughly enjoying themselves, including Dick.'

'I still can't see why Patricia didn't arrange it in an orthodox way, a proper party with party dresses, and the children sitting round the table.'

'Because it's Peggy's birthday and this is the way she wanted it,' said Charles. 'Actually, she wanted a *braaivleis* in the evening, but as some of her guests are a little young for that, she compromised, and agreed to have a picnic tea in the garden. By the way, Lorraine, I suppose you were invited?'

Lorraine was silent.

'Weren't you?'

'Well, not in so many words, but as I was told it was to be an informal do, I thought it wouldn't matter if I tagged along with Dick.'

'So you can hardly grumble about the form the party

takes, can you? David!' Charles caught hold of David, who was running about with another small boy, making zooming noises and pretending to be jet planes. ' Run and get Mrs Jorgens a chair, will you? She doesn't like sitting on the ground. There's a good chap.'

Peggy, who had gone into the kitchen with Patricia to supervise the lighting of the candles on her birthday cake, looked pathetically at Patricia.

' Why did *she* have to come?' she asked. ' She wasn't invited, and I'm sure Dick didn't want her tagging along either. She'll spoil everything. Oh, I know she gave me those lovely handkerchiefs, but she's not the sort of person to come to a party like this. She'll be grumbling all the time, or saying nasty things about people. You know what she's like.'

Privately, Patricia thought it was big of Peggy to say the handkerchiefs were lovely. Lorraine had presented Peggy with a little box containing two minute and very cheap-looking handkerchiefs in the manner of a queen conferring an accolade.

' She won't spoil anything, Peggy,' she said. ' She won't worry with the children or the games. You know she doesn't much like children. We'll keep her out of your hair. You see, she won't worry you at all.'

' Pat, you're simply fantabulous!' Peggy hugged Patricia and gave her one of her rare kisses—a rather sticky kiss as she had already been eating jelly and trifle.

' Run along now,' said Patricia, absurdly touched. ' Minah and I are bringing your cake any minute, and you must be in your place when it comes out.'

Peggy was in her place just in time. The cake was borne out and put in front of her, and she managed to blow out all the candles at once, to the tune of cheers and applause, aided by a little breeze that sprang up at exactly the right moment. The cake was cut and handed round, Lorraine accepting a minute portion which she ate fastidiously before wiping her fingers on a scrap of lace.

The party, naturally, was a pretty noisy one, but at one moment there was a lull in which Lorraine could be heard plaintively remarking that she was parched, and when was the tea coming.

'Tea?' asked Richard, turning round from the place of honour next to Peggy. 'There's not going to be tea. This isn't that kind of a party. Have a cool drink.'

He neatly decapped a bottle containing an acid-green liquid, reached for the straws, stuck two in and handed it to Lorraine, who shuddered.

'You know I can't drink that stuff,' she said.

'Sorry. That's all there is,' said Richard unsympathetically.

'I'll make you some tea if you like, Mrs Jorgens,' said Patricia, getting nimbly to her feet. 'I'm going in to get the rest of the ice-cream anyway.'

'You stay where you are, Pat,' said Richard. 'Lorraine, if you want a cup of tea as badly as all that, I'll run you back to the hotel.'

'You're not going?' Peggy's voice was almost a wail.

'It's all right, Peg-top; I'll be coming right back,' said Richard. Seeing that she was pacified, he propelled Lorraine up the garden and into the house.

It had been perfectly true that Patricia had intended going to fetch some more ice-cream, but she had not wanted to cross the garden in Lorraine's company. When she was sure that Richard must have got her well away, she went up to the house and into the kitchen by a back door that did not lead into the hall. She had opened the deep-freeze and taken out the bucket that contained the remainder of the ice-cream, and was just going to ladle some into a bowl from which it would be easier to serve it, when she realised that Lorraine and Richard were still in the house.

In point of fact, they were in the hall, and as the kitchen door was ajar, Patricia could hear every word that they were saying. They were having a quarrel.

'I'm certainly *not* staying down at the hotel with you,' Richard was saying, quietly but firmly.

'But I don't want to have tea there all alone. There's hardly anyone there on a Saturday afternoon, and the ones that are there are a ghastly crowd of old fuddy-duddies,' said Lorraine petulantly.

'Well, you ought to have made yourself other arrangements for this afternoon,' pointed out Richard reasonably. 'You've known since yesterday afternoon that I was coming to Peggy's birthday party this afternoon. You knew it was going to be a children's party, but you insisted upon gate-crashing. The least you could do is to join in the fun and not spoil things for Peggy.'

'But it was because I couldn't raise anyone that I wanted to come with you, Dick,' protested Lorraine. 'All the bridge fours were made up, and the tennis club's much too good for me; I was never any good at ball games. Honestly, there's nothing doing at the week-end in a one-eyed little dorp like this.'

'Then why stay here? And why, as I've asked before, gatecrashing into a party that you know isn't going to be your kind of a do?'

'I didn't know it was going to be quite as bad as it is.'

'Then, for heaven's sake, Lorraine, what did you expect?'

'The children sitting round a table in party clothes. I knew I'd be bored to tears, but I did think I'd be able to sit up to a table and have a decent cup of tea. Anyway, it would have been better than stuffing away alone down at that lousy hotel. Honestly, Dick, that girl's no use at all.'

'What girl?'

'Patricia Lang. I can't see why you employed her.

Someone older and more responsible would have been much better. Imagine organising a birthday party where the guests all sit round on a groundsheet in the garden and drink those horrible mineral waters out of the bottle. It's just downright lazy, that's what it is!'

'I've told you before, Lorraine, Peggy wanted that kind of a party; it was much more fun for them than having to sit politely round the table and being careful of their best clothes. That may be all very well in the winter, but it's far better for them to enjoy themselves outside in the summer. I never heard of anything so stupid. And as for hinting that Pat's lazy—the idea's ridiculous. Now come on and let's get you back to the hotel for your tea or I'll never get back to the party.'

'I don't see why you've *got* to come back to the wretched party.' Lorraine's voice had become petulant.

She'll never get him that way, thought Patricia, frozen at the kitchen table for fear of letting them know that she was overhearing. If only she had moved—made a noise—as soon as she had heard them, they might have gone and talked somewhere else. It was too late now, though. She would just have to wait until they had finished their argument. She wished to goodness that they would hurry up.

'I've got to come back because I promised Peggy I would,' said Richard, 'and because she wants me to and it's her birthday.'

'I don't see that that's so important,' replied Lorraine.

'Don't you? I happen to think that it's very important to keep a promise, especially to a child.'

'And as for the way you keep on sticking up for the Lang girl—' said Lorraine waspishly. 'You won't hear a word against her. Anyone'd think you were in love with the child, and what is she? A little waif you picked up in Capetown—a connection of the man who embezzled thousands.'

'Shut up, Lorraine, and come *on*!' It sounded as though Richard had taken Lorraine's arm, or was in some way or other, propelling her forcibly towards the front door.

'I believe you *are* in love with her, Dick,' taunted Lorraine. Richard's answer was inaudible as by that time they were going through the front door. A second later Particia heard it slam, and in the distance Richard's car driving off. She was glad that he would not be back for quite a while. It would give her hot cheeks a chance to cool off. The children would not notice that her colour was twice as high as it usually was.

Richard was not away very long, and from his manner no one would have known that he had been involved in a rather nasty argument with a trouble-making woman. Patricia was sure now, as she watched him organising games for the birthday guests, that he was unlikely to be ensnared by Lorraine. For one thing, he was too wily, and for another, she had shown her hand too soon and too unpleasantly. Richard was genuinely fond of his sister's orphaned children, and he intended to care for them to the best of his ability. To help do that, he had employed Patricia, and as far as she knew, she was giving satisfaction. She knew that he was *not*, in fact, in love with her, as Lorraine had suggested, but she wished with all her heart that he was. She told herself that she was happy for him, that he did not seem to be falling for Lorraine's blandishments, for she had thought all along that Lorraine could make no man happy, let alone a kindly, honest man such as Richard Horton.

The party began to break up at about six o'clock, when the mothers of the younger guests—those who had not stayed with their offspring, began to come and fetch them home. Although the older ones continued to play, the party spirit was not the same. The children began to tire, and when, at half past seven, the last guest went home, even Peggy sighed with relief.

To Peggy's and Patricia's delight, and Patricia's surprise, Richard stayed to a supper of left-overs, and helped to wash up afterwards, Minah having gone home long ago. Afterwards, Peggy was not reluctant to seek her bed. School sports one day and a lively birthday party the following day had tired her out. Richard and Patricia enjoyed a companionable cup of coffee on the back stoep when she had gone to her room.

' You've been here quite a time, Pat,' said Richard, ' and you seem to have settled in very well. Are you liking the job?'

' Loving it,' she said simply.

' I wonder why.' He spoke quietly and thoughtfully. ' It's not much of a job really. It doesn't need any specialised knowledge; it's not particularly interesting. You spend most of your time with two children, neither of them really old enough to meet you on equal terms, but you never seem bored with their company. Another thing; in spite of your domestic science training, which you tell me was a very short one, and the fact that you looked after your aunt's children occasionally, you've had no real experience of running a house and being in sole charge of three children, yet you're doing it as though you'd never done anything else.'

Patricia glowed. ' I was scared stiff at first,' she confessed. ' I don't know what I'd have done without Mary Milstead's help and advice. It's only the last month or two that I've really felt properly settled and as though I know what I'm doing. Before that, I would run next door for everything, unless I ran for the doctor instead.'

Richard laughed. ' The time Peggy fell out of the loquat tree, for instance?'

' Exactly. As for being bored—I love the children. They're darlings. And I have adult company. Mary

168

and I are always in and out of one another's houses, and I often go and spend an afternoon or evening with Maggie van der Berg. Now I've got the car, I'll be able to take the children out to the Scotts' farm. Every time I meet Erica, she asks me, but up to now I've always had to wait until the Milsteads are going too, for a lift, or for Erica to be in town when she can take us back with her. Yes, I've plenty of adult company as well as being with the children.'

'It seems that my hunch came off, then?'

'It just *had to*! Look, Richard, against all sense and reason, you took me on and gave me this job. Yet you'd caught me out in a stupid bit of deceit. Oh, I don't suppose it would have done any great harm if it had gone on, though I'd never have agreed to do it if I'd not been pretty desperate. But instead of throwing me out, or turning me over to the police, you gave me this job—a job with a home. I've never really had a home before, Richard; not since I was almost too small to remember. I've always been either staying with Granny or spending the long holidays out here with Mummy and Uncle Garth. I never really felt at home in Uncle Garth's house, although when I had left school and was more or less grown-up, I had lots of fun.

'I had a sickener of that kind of fun, though, after the crash. Most of our friends melted away. There were only types like Simon, who kept on being friendly because he could use me although I hadn't any money.'

'Well, I'm glad you're happy, Pat. I shouldn't like to think I'd pushed you into something you hated, and if you're happy, you'll make the children happy. And go on writing me letters about them. I like your letters, Pat. You certainly have the gift of putting things on paper and making them come alive.' Richard heaved himself to his feet. 'Well, pleasant as it is out here, I suppose I'd better get back to the Van der Bergs' place.

I don't want to keep them up too late.'

' You're—you're not stopping at the hotel, then?'

' No. It's comfortable enough, and I do often put up there, not wanting to impose too much on my friends, but when Maggie and Paul are as pressing as they were this weekend, I can't refuse. Well, goodnight, Pat. I may see you at church tomorrow; if not, it's goodbye for the present as I've got to leave tomorrow after lunch. I've a business contact to make on the way home.'

Patricia went to the front door with him, and watched his car round the corner. She did not go back into the house until his tail-light had disappeared round the corner, then she went thoughtfully to wash up their coffee cups. He may not be in love with me, she thought. Although I wish he could be, it would be very surprising if he were. But at least I know he's satisfied with the way I'm looking after the children, and he seems to like me for myself. That's better than nothing.

She went to bed happy.

Lorraine appeared to efface herself for the first half of the week, which was unusual. On Wednesday afternoon, coming home from the school swimming bath, Peggy, on her new bicycle, went into a dry skid on a patch of gravel just outside the hotel, and as luck would have it, Lorraine happened to be coming out just at that moment.

She did nothing; that would be most unlike Lorraine Jorgens. She waited, however, to see if Peggy was badly hurt. It seemed as though the child suffered nothing worse than a grazed knee, though she seemed somewhat shaken. A school-friend was with her, and helped her to her feet. She seemed able to walk all right, and appeared more concerned about her bicycle than she was about her own injuries. When the two girls had ascertained that it was not damaged other than for a scratch or two on its new paint, they pushed their bicycles and walked towards Green Street, for the way was uphill and the afternoon hot.

Lorraine smiled to herself, and went to call upon Maggie van der Berg.

Later that evening, Mary Milstead said to her husband, 'Keep an eye on Peter for a while, dear. Maggie's just rung, and I want to go over and see Pat. Someone saw Peggy come off her bike this afternoon. I want to go and see if she's all right. You know how Pat worries.'

'Right. He's asleep, isn't he?' About to return to his book, Charles looked up again. 'If it was Peggy they saw coming off her bike, why didn't Maggie ring Pat direct instead of you?'

'Tell you later. I want to get round to Pat's. It seems Lorraine had a hand in it, and Maggie didn't want to upset Pat. Lorraine seems to have been being more than usually poisonous.'

'Lorraine's never more than usually poisonous,' said Charles. 'She's just poisonous, full stop. How are you going to find out what happened without letting Pat know? After all, you've heard yourself through a second person. Won't Pat think it odd?'

'I shan't tell her; she'll tell me. I'm going to ask her if she's still got Tant' Min Venter's recipe for pineapple *confyt*.'

'*Slim*, aren't you?' said her husband admiringly. '*Slim*' is the Afrikaans word for sly, wily or crafty. 'All right, darling. I'll hear all about it when you get back. 'Bye now. I hope Peggy wasn't too badly damaged.'

'I hardly think so, or we'd have heard about it before now. Pat would have been in herself.'

'Too true.' Charles went back to his book, keeping an ear open for his baby son.

Patricia came to the door as soon as Mary knocked.

'Come in. How lovely to see you. I was longing for the excuse to make a cup of tea.' Patricia drew her inside. Mary told her why she had come—the official reason.

'Of course. I'll copy it out for you while the kettle's boiling.'

Mary bided her time, knowing that Patricia would say something about the accident in good time. She was right.

'It's nicer outside on the stoep, I know,' said Patricia, bringing in the tea-tray, 'but we'll have it in here if you don't mind.' She put the tray down on the low table in the comfortably shabby lounge. 'Peggy came off her bike this afternoon. She gave her knee a nasty graze, but she was more worried about the paint on her bike. I know I sound like a hen with one chick and children will knock themselves about, but she did have a bit of a shock, and I'd like to be within earshot, and her room's in the front of the house.'

'Poor little Peg, how bad is it?' asked Mary sympathetically.

'Just a graze really. I think I got all the dirt out. I put some of that yellow stuff Paul gave us when David skinned his knees falling off the Van der Mescht children's swing. I rang him and asked him if he thought she needed anti-tetanus serum, and he said no; she only had some a month ago when she cut herself on the garden hoe.' Pat took a deep draught of tea. 'I needed that!'

'Honestly, Pat!' Mary laughed, but kindly, not scornfully. 'You worry too much. I hate to think what you'd do if something really bad happened to the children. If it did, though, it wouldn't be your fault. Just take care, though, and don't let them see you're worried.'

'I don't think I do that,' said Patricia. 'I try not to. It's so bad for them; almost worse than not having enough care. I do try to make them independent and not smother them, but I can't help remembering that they're not mine, and that I'm responsible to Richard for their welfare.'

'If he doesn't know how well you look after them after the way I've sung your praises,' said Mary, 'then I just don't know.'

Patricia blushed a fiery red. 'Have you really, Mary? I'm always afraid he thinks I'm too young and feckless, though he was sweet about the way I look after them last time he was here—last weekend, after Peg's birthday party.'

'You think a lot of Richard, don't you, Pat?' asked Mary.

'To quote Peggy,' said Patricia lightly, 'I think he's fantabulous!'

'That's what I thought,' said Mary. 'It seems Lorraine thinks so too.'

'He—he wouldn't marry her, would he, Mary?' asked Patricia. 'I know he's perfectly capable of choosing a wife for himself if he wants one, but I'd hate him not to be happy; he's such a honey, and I'm sure Lorraine wouldn't make him happy.'

'I'm sure he wouldn't,' said Mary. 'We were all a bit worried at one time, when she first started chasing him. She's a fool, though. She shows her hand too soon, and she's too quick at showing that she's bored with things and people that he likes. Look out for her, though, Pat. She's vindictive and can make things unpleasant for people she thinks can put a spoke in her wheel. She's jealous of you, you know.'

'Of—of me? But she's got no reason to be jealous of me.' Patricia was dumbfounded.

'She seems to think she has,' said Mary. 'Still, she

can't do you any harm, so don't worry.'

Privately, Mary thought that if Lorraine wanted Richard—she did not say that Lorraine was in love with Richard, for she felt that Lorraine was incapable of loving anyone but herself—then she had ample reason to be jealous of Patricia. She was sure that the younger girl was deeply in love with Richard, and if he did not love her yet, then he was on the verge of doing so, and if Lorraine tried to put him against her, the effect would probably be to push him into Patricia's arms, but Lorraine would probably have made things so unpleasant for Patricia before that happened that the child might be frightened to accept him.

With a further word of reassurance, and thanking Patricia for the recipe, she said goodnight and took her leave.

On Thursday morning, Peggy cycled to school with a rather stiff knee, which was swathed in bandages. She happened to meet Lorraine when she was on her way home to lunch, which was not surprising, as Lorraine had lain in wait, sitting pretending to read on the hotel stoep until the children came out of school at the lunch hour.

'Hello,' she said, 'what have you done to yourself?'

Peggy, who was always excessively polite to people whom she disliked, said, 'Good morning, Mrs Jorgens. I skidded yesterday on my bike and grazed my knee.'

'You want to be careful,' said Lorraine solemnly. 'It can be nasty, falling off your bike. I'm surprised at Miss Lang, allowing you to ride to school alone on it.'

'But I'm eleven, Mrs Jorgens,' protested Peggy. 'I'm old enough to ride to school on my own. Children of nine cycle to school by themselves. It's not as though we lived far away, or out of town or anything, and Pat would never allow me out alone at night.'

'I should hope not!' Lorraine managed to sound

almost prim in her disapproval. 'Still, she's very young, isn't she? A little too young to have the care of three children. I don't think the discipline can be as good as if you had an older woman to look after you.'

'We like her,' said Peggy stoutly. 'We do what she wants us to because we love her, not because she has to punish us. I must go now, Mrs Jorgens, or Pat'll worry if I'm late. Goodbye.'

She rode off uphill, anger giving her legs strength to take her up the steepish road. She would not, she decided, say anything to Pat. It would only upset her. Patricia had never said anything against Mrs Jorgens to the children, but Peggy sensed that there was no love lost between the two women.

Patricia's next visitor was Lorraine herself. Lorraine had watched until she saw the little green Mini drive up past the hotel on its way from the town to Green Street, and had set off on foot, cursing herself for not bringing her car to Blouvlei. There had been method in her madness. Richard was spending more of his weekends in the dorp since he had installed Patricia as housekeeper and in charge of the children, and if he knew that she —Lorraine—had transport of her own, he would not offer her half so many lifts. It was a nuisance, though, when one wanted to get somewhere on a hot morning like this.

She arrived at an inopportune moment. Minah was peeling the potatoes, and Patricia was locking away the stores that she had brought back from town, and putting out the things that Minah would need. When the front doorbell rang, she jumped. Who could be calling at this hour? It was too late for morning tea.

'All right, Minah,' she said, for the maid was wiping her hands on her apron. 'I'll see who it is.'

Somehow, even after a walk uphill on a hot day, Lorraine managed to look cool and smart. She made

Patricia, in a rather crumpled cotton frock, feel grubby and very young. She waited, looking rather scornful at such gaucheness until Patricia recovered from her surprise enough to invite her inside.

'Would you rather tea, coffee or a cool drink?' she asked, when her guest was seated in the lounge. 'I'm afraid I can't offer you anything stronger.'

Lorraine looked surprised. 'I won't have anything, thanks. I'd have thought, though, after your gay life in Capetown, you'd have kept a spot in the house.'

'I was never much of a drinker even in those days,' said Patricia. 'I could never keep up with the crowd. Now, I feel I oughtn't to afford it—unless, of course, I want to give a party, but with prices going up, not as a general rule.'

'Why not?' asked Lorraine. 'You're paid well enough, I imagine. And you have your own car. I heard Richard tell you myself that you could use it for private outings as well as for the children.'

None of this, thought Patricia, was any business of Lorraine Jorgens'—however, if she was trying to make out that Richard's money was not being put to proper use, it would not help to try to snub her or to tell her to mind her own business.

'It's mainly for use with the children,' she said, 'and for bringing the shopping home, and that kind of thing. I use it very seldom for my own concerns. Even so, I pay for most of the upkeep out of my salary, which is more than generous. Apart from that, seeing that the household money's supposed to be for the upkeep of the house and the care of the children, I don't spend that on drink, and I'm trying to save as much of my salary as I can. Obviously, this job won't go on for ever. I won't be needed once the children are grown up, and as I'm not trained for any of the skilled professions, I'd be stupid not to save while I can, in case

I don't get as good a job when I have to look for something else.'

'You don't think of getting married, then?' asked Lorraine.

'I've no one in view at the moment,' replied Patricia, wondering where all this was leading to.

'Funny,' said Lorraine. 'I had an idea you had your eye on Richard.'

'Richard?' To her annoyance, Patricia felt her colour rising. 'Why, he would never think of me in that way. He's much older than I am, and anyway, I'm just a sort of glorified nursery governess.'

'I'm glad you realise that, my dear,' said Lorraine. 'In that case, why the blush?'

Patricia said nothing, and Lorraine went on: 'In spite of your innocent little ways and your denials of anything between you, I think you're in love with him, and I don't trust you. You see, I know your background and what your father was. Heredity will out.'

'What do you mean?' Patricia was at last stung into showing her indignation. 'I think you'd better be careful, Mrs Jorgens. My father was a most respectable schoolmaster. He died when I was five, but I lived with my grandmother—his mother—all the term-time when I was at school, and I know what kind of family he came from.'

'Of course, Garth Verity was your stepfather, wasn't he?' Lorraine was not in the slightest taken aback by Patricia's vehemence. 'It doesn't say much for your mother, does it, marrying a type like Garth Verity for her second husband.'

'I think we'll leave my mother's name out of this, Mrs Jorgens. When she married my stepfather, none of this had happened. I was assured by her greatest friend that she'd known nothing of what was going on, and it's my business in any case.'

'Of course, it would suit you down to the ground to get yourself a well-off husband, wouldn't it?' asked Lorraine. 'I know you're in love with Richard, so you needn't bother to deny it. I warn you, though, leave him alone; he's mine. He's far too old for you! Why, do you think he'd look at a chit of a girl like you?'

'I've never thought he'd be likely to "look at" me, as you put it.' In spite of her youthful appearance, Patricia was capable of immense dignity when she cared to exercise it. 'I think you've gone too far, Mrs Jorgens. I'm here to do a job of work, and I'm doing it to the best of my ability.'

'Letting the children fall off their bicycles and break their necks falling out of trees, I suppose.'

'Richard knows all about those accidents. I've always kept him informed of whatever happens to the children. I write a report every week.'

'I'll bet you do! Nice newsy letters that keep you in his mind, putting everything in a rosy light so that he thinks nothing is as serious as it really is.'

'Nothing of the kind. And I always get Dr van der Berg's opinion if anything's wrong. I rang him up about Peggy's knee when she fell off her bike, if that's what's worrying you.'

'It's not *worrying* me.' Patricia did not like Lorraine's smile. 'It'll come in very useful to me if I want to try and get Richard to see you as—shall we say as I'd like him to think you really are!'

Patricia hesitated for a split second, then remembered that the letter notifying Richard of Peggy's fall from her bicycle was already in the post, and that if he had not already received it, he would have it that afternoon.

'I've already informed him of that,' she said, 'and of the steps I took to make sure that it was not serious.'

'*You* informed him! By the time I've finished, *your* word won't carry much weight. Oh no, he won't hear

178

anything from me; I was stupid enough to let him see that I'm not fond of children and that I don't like you. He's idiotically loyal to his employees, is Richard. But there are other ways of telling people things than by going straight to them. Ever heard of a whispering campaign?'

'I think you'd better go, Mrs Jorgens,' said Patricia, still somehow managing to appear dignified although her knees were shaking and her lips were stiff. 'I haven't much time for malicious threats.'

'Yes, I'll go now,' said Lorraine. 'Please don't bother to see me out.'

CHAPTER XII

When Lorraine had gone, Patricia went almost auto-
matically out on to the back stoep and stared unseeingly
across the veld to the blue mountains beyond, but for
once the quiet veld had no power to soothe her. All she
could see was Lorraine's mocking fox-face with its
yellow-green slanted eyes and russet crown, which this
morning had been parted in the centre and brushed up
until it really did almost look like a fox's pointed ears.

She did not mind going to others for advice about the
children, but preferred to fight her own battles alone. This
one, however, was beyond her, and it could involve the
children if Lorraine really did as she had threatened to do
—blackened her name with Richard through other people.

She instructed Minah briefly to keep an eye on Podge,
who was in a larger, sturdier playpen than the one that
he had learned to overturn a month or two ago, and to
tell the other two, if they came home from school before
she got back, that she would not be long, and then she
slipped through the garden fence to the Milsteads' and,
finding Mary alone, for Charles was busy in his study,
she poured out the whole of the interview.

'How ridiculous!' exclaimed Mary when the tale was
done. 'You mustn't let it worry you, Pat. What can
that creature do to harm you? Of course Richard knows
what good work you've done. Has he ever complained
about the household accounts? Don't the children
always look healthy and well-dressed?'

Pat managed a small smile. 'I wouldn't say they
were particularly well-dressed last week at Peggy's
party,' she said.

'Well, you know what I mean,' said Mary. 'They're
obviously well cared for, and their clothes are always

in good repair.'

'She said she'd see that Richard knew about Peggy's grazed knee,' said Patricia. 'Of course, I told her I'd written to him about that, and she didn't like it because I've been writing to him. How else could I let him know about the children, Mary? I know he's up here fairly often, but not regularly. I have to let him know what's going on!'

'She's a bit stupid if she's thinking of trying to put him against you through the children,' said Mary.

'That was just it,' said Patricia. 'She admitted that she had been stupid to let him see that she wasn't fond of children and didn't like me, so she knew it wasn't any good going directly to him, and then she asked me if I'd never heard of a whispering campaign. She looked horrible when she said it, Mary; just like a fox.'

'The little—!' Mary bit off a word. Then, 'Look, Pat,' she said, 'what can she do? All that she can possibly do is to go round the dorp spreading mud, and what mud is there to spread about you? I should think you're unique. You're a young, pretty girl, and you've been in Blouvlei for more than four months without there having been any scandal about you. No one'll believe anything she has to say against you. No one!'

'D-do you really think so? I gathered that her idea was to put people against me by criticising the way I look after the house and children so that other people write and tell Richard that I'm not as satisfactory as he thought. He may not believe Lorraine Jorgens, but he might believe some of the more respected people of the district.'

'Who'd bother to go to all the trouble of writing to tell Richard what she says?' asked Mary. 'No, the worst that would happen might be that a few of the more catty types would have a natter over the teacups or the bridge table, and then forget all about it as soon as the next more juicy scandal came up.'

Eventually, much calmed, Patricia went back through the garden fence to give Peggy and David their lunch. They did not notice that she ate little herself, but took more time than usual feeding Podge. She was a little quieter than usual, but there was nothing in her manner that could tell the two older children that she had had a mortal shock.

'I don't like it, Mary,' said Charles Milstead as his wife repeated what Patricia had told her as they ate their lunch. 'Lorraine Jorgens is a dangerous woman.'

'But what can she do, darling?' said Mary.

'Make things darned unpleasant, if nothing worse,' said Charles.

. Mary repeated what she had said to Patricia about the subject being discussed over the bridge tables until a more interesting item of gossip appeared, but Charles looked grave.

'It's that threat of a whispering campaign that I don't like,' he said. 'I'm sure Lorraine won't get Richard; she's thrown herself at his head too hard, and let him see too many of her bad points too soon—'

'Has she any good ones?' interpolated his wife.

'But she's not quite a fool,' went on Charles as though she had not spoken. 'She may not realise that she's lost him herself, but she's clever enough to put him against Pat. She's a past master of the whispering campaign that she mentioned to Pat. Pat was quite right to be frightened of it. You weren't here when she nearly wrecked things for Nick and Fiona Shaw. It was in Boschfontein—the next district. We heard *all* about it here in Blouvlei. Nick's first wife was Lorraine's sister, and just as bad as Lorraine. When Lorraine's divorce came through, she came and parked herself at the Shaws' place, Witvlerke. Nick's old grandmother was still alive then, and very old and very frail. Fiona was some distant connection of old Mrs Shaw and had come out from Scotland when her own home broke up when someone died. The old lady thought the world of her.

'Lorraine stayed on when old Mrs Shaw died of a heart attack, her excuse that she was needed as a chaperon, and couldn't leave until Fiona went, as she couldn't leave a young girl alone on the farm with Nick. Of course, she was after him herself, and she quietly spread the most ghastly rumours about the place until Fiona couldn't stand it any more, and did a bunk. Nick wouldn't turn her out; she was a family connection without a relative in the world but him. She's an independent Scot, though, and a trained nurse. She could always earn her living if she had to.

'Well, by the time Lorraine had finished, even here in Blouvlei, we'd heard so much that we were wondering what kind of a woman old Mrs Shaw's paragon had turned out to be. No one outside the family ever knew what the last straw was, but it seems that Fiona planned everything in advance, booked her seat on the train, and left for Cookhouse, via the siding; got a lift in the truck with the boy when he took the milk cans in. I think she was making for Aloe Bay. She left a note in her room for Nick, telling him she couldn't stand it any longer, but not letting him know where she was going. He only found out from Ann Fraser, Dr Fraser's wife, who was a friend of Fiona's. It was Mike Fraser's sister in Aloe Bay who'd asked Fiona to stay there.

'Nick caught her up at Cookhouse by the skin of his teeth, brought her home, kicked Lorraine out, and married Fiona before she could run away again.

'Fiona was a trained nurse of about twenty-four or five, who'd already survived a broken engagement, or a fiancé being killed or something over in Scotland, but had a solid background with a Scottish grandmother or something, and she was nearly stampeded by Lorraine. Pat's twenty-one, and in spite of a bit of sophistication, which has nearly worn off since she's been here, a young twenty-one, except for her sense of responsibility towards those kids. She's never had a proper home—been shuttled back and forth for most of her life between her grandmother and her stepfather's home—two totally different kinds of environment. It beats me how she's turned out as good as she has.

'Then the shock of losing her mother and stepfather, and learning that her stepfather was a crook and finding herself with no money and no training to help her earn a living. I'd say she was a sitting target for *dear* Lorraine to shoot at, and a whispering campaign is one of the most difficult things to fight.'

By the time he had finished this long speech, Mary looked as grave as he did.

'What can we do?' she asked.

'Wait and see what happens, and play it off the cuff,' said Charles. 'We've got a pretty good standing in the neighbourhood. Dad was pretty well-known—a national figure with his books.'

'So are you,' said Mary.

'So much the better. We must be seen as much as possible with Pat. We must befriend her as much as we can, and if we hear anything against her, we must be indignant when we deny it. We must warn Maggie and Paul too. Our line must be if people like the Milsteads and the Van Der Bergs have taken the girl up, there can't be so very much wrong with her. Don't forget, Maggie's Josephine Cantrell, a minor celebrity in her own right.'

'I knew you'd think of something,' said Mary.

'It's not going to be easy,' her husband warned her.

· · · · ·

At first, nothing much was heard. The thing only snow-balled gradually, but Lorraine had immense patience. By the end of March, some of the older women were stopping Patricia while she was out shopping and asking if she thought it wise to bring Podge out in all weathers.

'I don't,' she said. 'I left him at home last week when there was that thunderstorm, but I feel safer about him when he's with me than if I leave him alone at home with the maid, and although our next-door neighbour, Mrs Milstead, has said she'll always keep an eye on him, I don't like to presume too much on her kindness. After all, she has a good deal to do of her own, and I am being paid to look after the children.'

The old lady appeared satisfied.

A few days later, Peggy came home from school full of indignation.

'What d'you think?' she asked. 'Dominee du Preez asked me if I was always allowed to tear about to and from school alone. I told him that most of the eleven-year-olds went to school alone on their bikes unless they lived too far away. Isn't he stupid?'

Patricia's heart sank. Lorraine had indeed been busy, if the Dutch Reformed Church *Predekant* was taking a critical interest in the children's welfare.

The wife of the Methodist Minister stopped her one morning and asked her if she didn't think that David was a little too young to be allowed to go to school on his own. After all, she pointed out, he was not yet seven.

'But he doesn't go on his own,' protested Patricia. 'He meets a friend on the corner, and goes down with him and his mother, and besides, the junior boys' school's only just round the corner from Green Street.'

She took to cutting short her own breakfast and seeing David to the corner to make sure that he did, in fact, meet Jannie Korsten. She gave up all her own activities, and never went anywhere without the children. She refused to go out even when Mary Milstead offered to babysit for her.

'It's not that I don't trust you with the children, Mary,' she said. 'You know that. But if I'm seen out at a film or a dance or something, and Lorraine sees me, it'll be all round the place. If Richard hadn't had to go overseas on business, someone would have written to him about me by now, and that's for sure.'

Unwillingly, Mary had to agree that she was right. She was growing thin and pale, and looked older than her twenty-one years. She decided to pay a call on her sister-in-law, Maggie van der Berg.

'She'll crack up if she goes on like this,' said Mary, rescuing her son, who was just about to pull down a flower arrangement that Maggie had taken a long time to make. 'I'm worried, Maggie, but I don't know what we can do. As long as that Jorgens creature hangs about in Blouvlei, it'll go on.'

'If only Dick hadn't had to go to the U.K. and the States for the firm!' lamented Maggie.

'That's just what Pat said,' replied Mary, 'only she said that if he hadn't been overseas, someone would have been sure to have written to him by now. Yes, they're making remarks to her face now as well as behind her back.'

'As long as they all come back to us,' said Maggie, 'we can do a bit to counter them.'

'I'm swinging Charles's family's reputation for all I'm worth,' said Mary. 'Asking them if they think the Milsteads would take up anyone who wasn't one hundred per cent above board.'

'And I'm plugging Paul's reputation as the family doctor of the dorp, and his father's before him, saying I'm sure old man van der Berg would have liked her. Of course, I never knew the old man; he died when I was tiny, but I don't have to stress that.' Maggie grabbed her godson, picked him up and hugged him before he had time to pull the tea-table over.

'I think I'd better go before there's any damage done,' said Mary. 'This young man's getting restless.'

She wished that Richard was due back before the end of May. Patricia had refused even to let her babysit so that she could go and make her Communion on Easter Day. She had taken all three children with her to church, and David had been bored and Podge had chatted to himself all through the service. Only Peggy, who was going through a religious phase and wanted to be confirmed when she was twelve, had sat quiet, drinking it all in.

To her discomfiture, they had received some black looks from some of the other parishioners, but when she apologised to the Rector on her way out, he had brushed it aside saying that he wished that more people would start their children off on the right foot while they were young.

Patricia seemed to settle down in her somewhat dreary routine and to look a little better again. Mary and Maggie congratulated themselves on the fact that now that May had begun, the end of the month and Richard's return was not so far away now.

The days were long and mellow, but the mornings and evenings were chilly and crisp, the stars looking brighter and more numerous in the frosty mountain air.

One evening, early in May, Patricia, Mary and Maggie were all sitting in front of the first fires of the winter in their own respective homes, when the Milstead telephone rang.

'Oh, blow!' Mary put down her knitting and got up. 'All right, darling, I'll go. It's probably someone wanting to know if I'll make them *melkterts* for the church bazaar.'

She left the door open, and the door of the study, where the telephone stood. Charles heard her give their name and number, and then: '*Dick!* When did you get back?'

'This morning,' he told her. 'I got through quicker than I expected, and thought I'd surprise you all by turning up in Blouvlei, but I've been going through my mail, and I've found the most astonishing collection of letters from the dorp, mostly from people I've never heard of, trying to tell me that Pat's not a suitable person to look after Martha's children. What on earth is going on up there?'

'Well, as a matter of fact,' began Mary, 'Lorraine. . . .'

'That's what's so odd,' broke in Richard. 'Most of them mention Lorraine. What's she got to do with it, and since when has she been cultivating the churches? The Methodist Minister's wife, the *Dominee*, someone who signs herself Samantha Wotherspoon, and she says she's a pillar of the Blouvlei Anglican Ladies' Guild . . . I don't know who else. I tell you, I've not met one half of them.'

'Have you contacted Pat about it?' asked Mary.

'No, I haven't. I wanted to find out what it was all about without upsetting her, if I could help it.'

'Good boy!' Mary's exclamation was heartfelt.

'Yes, but what's it all about, Mary?' persisted Richard.

'Lorraine's jealous of Pat. She wants to marry you——'

'*Lorraine* does? But that's ridiculous! I spend most of my time when I'm with her trying to shake her off, or snubbing her because she keeps on being catty about Pat.'

'Don't you see, that's just it. She thinks you'd make an admirable husband number two, and she sees Pat as a threat to her plans. Poor Pat's the designing female who's out to catch you.'

'But that's absurd. Pat couldn't be a designing female if she tried. She's far too transparent.'

'That's just the trouble. Lorraine's been carrying out a whispering campaign against Pat, making out to other people that she's falling down on the job, because she knows you wouldn't listen to her. That's where she's been so clever. She's managed to get people like the Minister and the Predekand and old Sammy Wotherspoon of our Ladies' Guild to listen to her. The Van der Bergs and Charles and I have done our best to contradict the rumours, but Lorraine seems to have cast her net too wide for us to reach them all.'

'But the woman must be mad! They must all be mad to think that Pat doesn't look after the kids properly. Why, she's so afraid that she'll slip up that she worries about the most idiotic things! That's one of the things I love her for; the way she gets all steamed up when one of the kids scratches a knee or something.'

'You love her, do you, Dick?'

'Of course I do!'

'There's no of course about it. You'd better get up here and tell her so as soon as you can. She's eating her heart out for you here.'

'She is?'

'That's what I said.'

'Well, I'll have to go into the office tomorrow morning, but then I needn't go back before Monday. I don't know what time I'll be able to get away tomorrow; I may not be able to get there before supper time, but if you'll kindly get off the line, I'll put a call through to Maggie and Paul and see if they can put me up for a couple of nights till I get this sorted out.'

Mary laughed. 'I like that! Who put this call through in the first place? And we can put you up all

189

right, Dick. There's no need to make another trunk call.'

' I know you can, love, but Maggie's got more room. 'Bye now.' Richard rang off and Mary went back to tell Charles that it looked as if most of Patricia's troubles were over.

The next evening, Patricia was sitting in front of the electric heater in the lounge darning a pair of David's shorts and wondering how he could wear the seat into such enormous holes. It was a cold evening; winter was nearly on them, but it seemed wasteful to light a fire for one person. She heard a car stopping in the road outside, but hardly noticed it. It was probably someone visiting one of the neighbours.

There were flying footsteps up the garden path, and an urgent ring at the front door. Bewildered, she got to her feet. Who could be making such a noise at half past eight on a winter's night in this quiet street? She put the door on the chain before she slid back the bolts, and then she flung the door open wide, when she saw who stood there, smiling down at her.

' Got anything to eat?' he asked. ' I've had no supper, and I'm starving.'

' I don't think there's anything but eggs,' she said as he followed her into the kitchen. ' How would you like them? Poached, scrambled, boiled, omelette or fried with bacon?'

' I don't care a damn so long as I can look at you while I eat them,' he said, at which Patricia burst into tears.

Before she knew what was happening, she was in his arms, and he was talking nonsense words to her, trying to comfort her. At last she was quiet.

' Now,' he said, ' tell me what's wrong?'

' Do you believe I neglect the children?' she asked,

threatening to cry again.

'Don't be stupid, love,' he said. 'If anything you overdo it. They could do with a little healthy neglect now and then. Now I know all about it. Don't worry about it any more.'

He kissed her long and hard, and would have gone on longer, had not David, who had been woken by the disturbance, come out to see what was going on.

'Hello, Dick,' he said calmly. 'Why're you kissing Pat?'

'Because I want her to marry me,' said Richard.

Pat looked up, her eyes shining. 'Do you *really*?'

'Of course I do. Would I make it so public if I didn't mean what I was saying?' he asked. Then Peggy was with them.

'Are you and Dick really going to get married?' she cried, fair plaits flying as she danced round the kitchen table. 'How simply fantabulous!'

'But if you and Pat marry,' said David to Richard, 'will you take her away to live with you and send someone else here to us? We wouldn't like that.'

'Of course not; we'd all be together,' said Richard. 'The only reason I couldn't have you with me was because I didn't have a wife to look after me and you too, of course.'

By now, Patricia was feeling so happy that she dared to tease him. 'I believe you're only marrying me so that you've someone to look after the children all the time,' she said.

Richard put one finger under her chin and tilted her face up until she had to look at him.

'No, so that I can look after all four of you,' he said softly.

'Then that's all right,' said David. 'Come on, Peg; let's go back to bed.'

'That's right, old chap. I'll have lots to tell you in

the morning. And you, Pegtop. 'Night, love.'

It took time. Peggy would not go until she had given and received a rapturous kiss and a bear-hug from both Patricia and Richard. At last there was peace.

'What about my supper?' asked Richard.

A little voice floated down the passage.

'Wan' d'ink water. Wan' d'ink water,' it chanted.

'Well,' said Patricia as she saw Richard's resigned expression, 'did you expect our Podge to be left out of anything?'

Don't miss any of these exciting titles.

Complete and mail this coupon today!

Harlequin Reader Service

IN U.S.A.:
MPO Box 707, Niagara Falls, N.Y. 14302

IN CANADA:
649 Ontario St., Stratford, Ontario N5A 6W2

Please send me my FREE Harlequin Reader Service Catalogue.

Name _____

Address _____

City _____

State/Prov. _____ Zip/Postal _____

R1606

Don't let this chance pass you by!